IN THUG LOVE WITH A CHI-TOWN MILLIONAIRE

J. DOMINIQUE

In Thug Love With A Chi-Town Millionaire

Mailing List

To stay up to date on new releases, plus get information on contests, sneak peeks, and more,

Go To The Website Below...

www.colehartsignature.com

CHAPTER ONE
CA'MAHRI

This some bullshit! I thought to myself as I rocked a baby on my hip and watched the other one jump from couch to couch, screaming at the top of his lungs. The question of how I'd gotten myself in this situation rang in my head as I looked around at the mess they'd created in less than thirty minutes, and the answer came back loud and clear. Good dick. Good dick had me overlooking every red flag that came with that nigga, and now he was leaving me to babysit his rug rats while he made plays, in my car no less.

Walt definitely had good dick and knew how to use it too, thus the two bad ass kids from two different women that had destroyed my living room. He was so skilled that after only six months of dating, he'd sprung his kids on me along with their mammies and I was still around. However, knowing about some kids and babysitting them were two different things. I didn't understand how we'd gone from Netflix and chilling to me watching them until he came back to drop them off with their mamas or his mama or whoever. I'd been so discombobulated by the request that I didn't even know anymore. I wanted to be petty and tell him to take them along with his ass, but even I knew a drug transaction was no place for kids. The way they turned up after he left, though, had me ready to turn into Mya and start riding looking for his ass.

"Aye! Nuh uh! Get yo' lil' ass off there!" I shouted once I saw his son, Walt Jr., preparing to climb on my coffee table. The way his little face twisted up at me instantly had me feeling disrespected. He paused, never losing eye contact with me, and went to finish lifting his knee onto the glass like I hadn't said shit. "Boy, I will—!" My words were cut off as I bit into my bottom lip and yanked his bad ass down with my free hand.

The little fucker immediately fell out and began shrieking loudly like I'd really hurt him. Shocked wasn't even the word to describe how I was feeling. I'd barely touched him and he was writhing around on the floor, making my jaw drop, unsure of what to even do. His antics got his sister started right back up and suddenly, I had two screaming ass kids on my hands. Normally, I was pretty good with kids, especially toddlers, but these two were from a different planet.... or from the pits of hell, because I had no clue how to settle them down besides allowing them to fuck up my house. Their abandoned Happy Meals were still spread out across my hardwood floor, so it wasn't food they wanted and I didn't keep snacks around to even offer. I could feel a headache coming on as I pulled out my phone so I could text their daddy. Even though I hadn't done anything or asked to be his designated babysitter, I didn't want him to hear them fussing and think I'd done something, so I hurriedly let him know they were asking for him and he needed to bring his ass back!

I began to pace as I started back rocking his daughter, Willow, and waited on him to reply. A few seconds later, my phone was ringing and I answered without looking. "Hello."

"Girl, what the hell you got goin' on over there? It sounds like a damn daycare!" my sister questioned loudly in an effort to be heard over my background, and I rolled my eyes from the ridiculousness of the situation and because she wasn't Walt.

"It's a long story, but the short version is Walt left his kids here while he went to make a bip and they're some straight Bebe's." Instead of feeding into Jr.'s tantrum, I carried the baby over to my loveseat and plopped down so I could look through the Walmart bag that was doubling as a diaper bag for a pacifier or something to help. Unfortunately, there wasn't shit in there but a few diapers and some wipes. I couldn't do shit but shake my head, wondering what type of bitch only packed diapers and nothing else.

"Ewww, not you playin' stepmama!" she cracked, and I could hear the frown in her voice. My sister had a strict no niggas with kids rule that she lived by along with a bunch of other no-no's that had her extremely judgmental when it came to my dating life. Honestly, if I would've known it was her and not Walt, I definitely wouldn't have answered.

"It's only been like ten minutes," I lied, shooting a look at the kids, who still hadn't shut up.

"Biiiitch, I don't give a fuck if it was one minute! That nigga ain't have no business leaving them kids with you! I'm assuming this your first time meeting them, right?" her smart ass quickly guessed, making me feel even more stupid.

"I mean..." I dragged, rolling my eyes toward the sudden knocking at my front door.

"Yo' ass just meeting 'em! He'd have me so fucked up if I was you, and they're all loud and shit, probably got yo' house lookin' like a tornado ran through that bitch! Tuh!" she continued to rant, and I tuned her ass out as I carried the baby to the door, praying it was their daddy.

"Uhh, who is you and where Walt at?" My facial expression

matched that of the woman standing on my porch as her eyes bounced between me and Willow. Before I could recover from her appearing on my doorstep and process her first two questions, she'd snatched the baby from my arms and inspected her from head to toe. "Fuck you do to her for her to be crying like this? I swear Walt got me so fucked. Why would he leave my baby with you?"

"Hold up, I know that ain't the baby mama questioning you! Tell that bitch she better get her kids and get the fuck on —matter fact, I'ma tell her!" The phone beeped in my ear, indicating that Camille had hung up and was more than likely on her way.

"Okay, so first of all, I'ma need you to tone it down about four notches. I ain't yo' baby daddy, so whatever grievances you got, you need to take that shit up with him just like I'm 'bout to!" I snapped and slammed the door in her face before she could run her dick suckers anymore. I thought Walt was disrespectful for using me as a babysitter, but he was completely out of order to send his baby mama to my house! My hands shook furiously as I went to dial his number, ignoring that ignorant bitch outside still knocking. I figured if I ignored her she'd get the hint and go on about her business before I beat her ass. The fact that my call immediately went to voicemail after only ringing twice had me even more heated as I stomped back into the living room where Walt Jr. was now sitting up and kicking one of my end tables. I couldn't help wondering if he'd called his other baby mama for him or if he'd sent the one who'd just left for both kids, which pissed me off even more. Baby mama number two had me so caught off guard I'd forgotten all about his little bad ass, and now I was regretting being so quick to turn her away.

Letting out a low groan, I didn't even waste time yelling before just scooping him up in my arms and right on cue, the waterworks began. He was almost four so I wasn't about to be bouncing him around on my hip like I'd done his sister, so instead, I tucked him under one arm like they did the Chuckie doll all the time and went to find something to entertain him. Being that I didn't have kids, my apartment was void of any toys but I may have had an old teddy bear he could play with from Valentine's Day past. Anything to shut him up until I could find his daddy or figure something else out. I moved about my room, growing more frustrated as he continued kicking and shedding crocodile tears before finally finding a scruffy looking pink bear on the shelf in my closet.

"Oooh, look who I found! It's pinky the bear!" I told him in an overexaggerated voice, wiggling the bear in his face. The distraction worked for all of five seconds, before he chucked that motherfucker across the room, knocking my brand-new rose off its charger. The little red toy landed with a thud on the plush throw rug that sat right in front of my dresser and I winced, praying he hadn't broken it. True, Walt had been putting it down but it wasn't on a daily basis, so after seeing the reviews, I quickly ordered myself one for the times he wasn't available. It had just come the day before so I put it on the charger and left it to get as much juice as I could, and I was glad I did because it was going to come in handy after I beat Walt's ass and cut him off. Well, unless his son had broken it. I rolled my eyes at the thought and went to pick it up, praying that it still worked after this. As soon as I held the power button down, though, it immediately cut on and I breathed a sigh of relief. It took me a second to realize the loud vibrating had caught Walt Jr.'s attention, because he'd stopped crying and was now laser focused on the hand I was holding the toy in. My brows dipped as he reached for it and I had an internal battle with myself. On one hand, I didn't think it was appropriate to give his ass a sex toy just to shut up him up, but on the other, I was just about ready to try anything until his daddy returned. Unfortunately, the decision was made for me once his little ass started screaming again.

"TOOOOOYYY!"

"You know what, fuck it." I shrugged, placing it in his small hands, and he was immediately quiet again. His face lit up and any trace of tears vanished as he moved the toy from hand to hand in amazement.

"Girrrrrrl, I know damn well." My sister entered my room with a look of horror and amusement covering her face before she broke into a fit of giggles. Just like I knew she would, she'd put on her fighting gear and sped over, ready to fuck some shit up. Camille had shown up with her hair tucked in a scarf, clad in black leggings, a slightly fitted black t-shirt, and matching Timberlands that were tied tight, even though the baby mama was long gone by now.

"Look, whatever will shut him up 'cause at this point, he's giving me a headache," I explained, setting him down on the floor. With the toy still vibrating loudly, he was content and had even begun mocking the noise it was making.

"If you would've told his ass no out the gate then you wouldn't have no headache."

"I already know, Camille." I groaned, rolling my eyes. "It ain't shit I can do about it til' I find that nigga, tho', unless he send his other baby mama over here."

"I wish the fuck he would! I'm already pissed I missed the first one," her crazy ass said, folding her arms like she was really upset about missing the opportunity to fight somebody. "You know what, naw, we bouta go find his ass. Let's go, hoe! Grab yo' stepson!"

Ten minutes later, we were piled into her white 2020 Lexus with Walt Jr. strapped into the backseat. I'd been messing around with his daddy long enough to know a few of his hangouts and since he wasn't answering the phone for me, I was hoping we'd be able to catch his ass at one of them. It only took two guesses for us to find him out in front of the liquor store running his mouth while some other niggas shot dice nearby. He was so engrossed in his conversation that he didn't notice me until I was stomping toward him with his son on my hip. The closer I got, the more surprised his face became until they landed on Walt Jr.'s hands.

"Yo, what the fuck! Is that a fuckin' vibrator he holdin'?" he asked with his nostrils flaring, but he didn't have any right to be mad after leaving me with his kids to bullshit on the block. The people that were within hearing distance all tuned in at his question, as me and Camille came to a stop in front of him.

"Yep, and you owe me another one too since I didn't even get a chance to use it yet." With a smirk, I handed his son over to him, only being egged on by the chorus of laughter that erupted around us.

"Period!" Camille was thirsty to add from beside me.

"First of all, you lame as hell for leaving your kids with me just for you to be out here standing on the block! Then you sent yo' baby mama to my house like I know that bitch or somethin'! This is not that!" I clapped between each word. The longer I stood there the angrier I was getting, and I could see that he was as well just from the sheer embarrassment, but I wasn't the one that had put him in this situation.

"So, this what you do? You gon' bring yo' ass out here actin' a fool in front of all these niggas?" His jaw clenched as he stared down at me, and I released a chuckle. The moment was made even more funny because Walt Jr. was still playing with the different settings on the vibrator. He quickly smacked it out of his hands, causing his little bad ass to erupt into tears again.

"Yep, now run me my keys." I shrugged.

"Man, I ain't givin' yo' goofy ass shit! Get the fuck outta

here before I fuck you up!" I must admit that I was surprised at how quickly he'd switched up on me, but I was glad I hadn't gotten too invested in him to the point that this shit could hurt my feelings.

"Oh, I wish you would, ole bum ass nigga!" Camille chimed, preparing to fight him if necessary.

"Aye, y'all makin' shit hot as fuck right now. Give shorty her fuckin' keys before shit get ugly," a calm but deadly voice said, making everybody get quiet, and I locked eyes with the finest nigga I'd ever seen in my life. I'm talking tall, with smooth caramel skin and dark almost black eyes. Half his face was covered by a luscious beard and he had a ton of tattoos peeking up his neck. I'd been so focused on Walt when I walked up that I had completely missed him, but now that I'd laid eyes on his ass, I was stuck.

"My bad, D, I ain't—" One look from D had Walt swallowing the rest of his sentence and reaching down into his pocket to hand my keys over. That shit even had Camille quiet as a church mouse, and after mumbling a low thank you, we both got the fuck out of dodge. As scary as he was, though, I couldn't deny that he was on my mind long after I'd pulled away.

CHAPTER TWO

CAMILLE

"Hey Camille, Janice has a family emergency, so I need you to take her next couple patients until her replacement gets here." The head nurse Reyna stood over me just as I was about to take a bite of my salad. I really couldn't stand the bitch and I knew that she knew it too, which was why she always made it her business to bring me bad news. I was convinced she had purposefully come over at this moment just to ruin my meal, and I had to stop myself from cursing her out.

"Alright, Reyna," I said through clenched teeth, hoping that she'd carry her ass on, but she didn't move an inch.

"Ms. Banks is already here so you're gonna need to get a move on." She put on a phony smile before finally walking off, and I grit my teeth angrily. I'd literally just sat down on my break and hadn't even had time to do shit but put the dressing on my salad before she came fucking with me. Now my only option was to throw it away or stuff my mouth as I walked to the lab, which was a no-no. I'd been a phlebotomist at Rush

Hospital for the last five years and one thing I prided myself on was my professionalism at work. So instead of devouring my food like I wanted to, I went ahead and trashed it before making my way up to the fourth floor.

"Hey Camille," my work bestie, Noelle, spoke as soon as I rounded the nurses' station. She was one of the only people I fucked with at this hospital because she wasn't messy or a narc like a lot of the bitches they hired. Much like me, she kept to herself and minded her own business, which was why we got along so well. We'd even gotten together outside of work along with my sister, and outside of the hospital, she was just as ratchet as us too.

Smiling, I stopped to check the sign-in sheet as I greeted her. "Heeeey, I thought you was off today, girl," I quizzed in confusion. We'd talked the week before and I was pretty sure she wasn't supposed to be here until Wednesday, but nonetheless, I was happy to see her. Rolling her eyes, she leaned closer so nobody else could hear.

"I was. That bitch Kara called off *again*, so Reyna called me like it ain't fifty other people who could've came. I should've told her ass no, 'cause I really need to get my nails done." She looked at her hands sullenly.

"A shame, she just came and interrupted my lunch to take over for Janice. I ain't even get a bite of my shit." I sighed irritably just thinking about my wasted food. "I do need a fill tho' too, so if you want we can go after work. You can help me cheer up Ca'Mahri's ole heartbroken ass." Her brows instantly shot up because I hadn't told her about the shit that happened over the weekend.

"I thought Walt was a good one?"

"Tuh! He ain't shit just like the rest of 'em, but we gon' fill you in later, girl. Let me get in here and get Ms. Banks taken care of." Just thinking of how Walt's bum ass had tried to play my sister had me heated all over again. He was lucky that sexy nigga had stepped in when he did or he was going to get fucked up out there.

"Hmph! Well, you're in for a treat, boo, 'cause her grandson in there with her and he fine as hell, sis!" She grinned widely and wiggled her brows, making me laugh.

"I ain't fuckin' with you, girl. You know I keeps it professional at all times, I ain't studying her grandson."

"Okay, don't say I ain't warn you." With a shrug, she sat back in her seat, but the smile never left her face as I went to walk off. *Crazy ass heffa!* I wasn't going to pay her ass any mind. Wasn't no nigga fine enough to have me forgetting I was at work, and I had seen a few having been there so long. After the way she'd just hyped him up, though, I had to admit I was just a little curious, if for no other reason than to disagree with her pressed ass. I went and washed my hands before grabbing my cart and making my way to Ms. Banks's room. Knocking, I paused before entering backward so I could pull the big ass cart in.

"Hi, Ms. Banks. I'm Camille and...um." My brain went blank the moment I laid eyes on the brooding Adonis in the corner. Noelle had said the nigga was fine, but she hadn't really done his ass any justice. Even sitting down, I could tell he was tall as hell, with his long, bowed legs stretched out in front of him. His handsome caramel face was set in a scowl, but as soon as he realized the effect he was having on me, his lips separated into a cocky grin. I was a sucker for a nice smile and this nigga had a perfect set of straight white teeth that had me weak in the knees.

"Hey, baby, you okay?" Ms. Banks's voice snapped me out of the trance he had me in and I cleared my throat awkwardly, causing his grin to widen.

"Oh, ahem! Sorry about that, I'm okay. Mondays always

have me a little frazzled." I gave her a quick, reassuring smile, hoping my embarrassment wasn't evident on my face, before I began readying my supplies.

"I hope you get that shit under control before you pull out them needles then," Mr. Sexy commented icily, and my head snapped up to find his dark eyes on me. Now his face was emotionless, but the underlying threat was there and I instantly caught an attitude.

"Now Cash, be nice. I'm sure Camille can handle this….right, baby?" She gave her grandson a calming pat on the hand and looked at me with a raised brow. Biting the inside of my jaw, I managed a stiff nod.

"Yes ma'am, I'm *very* capable," I said with my eyes narrowed on her grandson. Just as fast as he'd caught my attention, he'd pissed me off. *Ole rude, arrogant nigga!* Ignoring him, I quickly and efficiently got the samples the doctor had ordered for Ms. Banks while making small talk with her. By the time I was finished, she was smiling and completely at ease like all of my patients.

"That was fast, baby! Usually, those girls be poking and prodding me in both arms before they finally get it right." She huffed like she was getting mad just thinking about it, and I couldn't help but chuckle. I knew exactly who she was talking about because we always got the same complaints about Janice and the other phlebotomist, Gina. It was no wonder they hadn't already been fired, but clearly the hospital wasn't going to be satisfied until somebody sued them behind those bitches' incompetence.

"Well, I'm glad you were able to get the best today." I winked at her with a warm smile before saying my goodbyes and slipping out of the room. As soon as I shut the door behind me, Noelle was right there with her arms folded, giving me a knowing look.

"So? He was fine as hell, right?" She fell into step beside me, ignoring my eyes rolling in irritation.

"Tuh! He was a rude asshole!" I growled, stopping to wash my hands before making my way back to the nurses' station so I could find out who my next patient was.

"But he was a fine, rude asshole, though, right?"

"He was ayite." I avoided her eyes and focused on the sign-in sheet.

"You're so full of shit." She scoffed, waving me off as she rounded the desk to sit down. "I'ma let you make it though."

"Girl, ain't nobody thinkin' 'bout that rude ass nigga!" I was lying through my teeth, because despite how he came at me in the room, his fine ass face was still etched in my memory. Normally, I wasn't pressed like this behind no nigga, but it was something about him that had him still on my mind.

Since the next patient on the sign-in sheet was marked off, I knew that Janice's replacement had finally arrived, which had me sucking my teeth. That bitch Reyna had made me rush up there and the girl had come within the ten minutes I'd been in with Ms. Banks. I shouldn't have even been surprised because she always pulled some bullshit when I worked with her, but playing with my food was something different. I fully intended on making her replace my salad, but a presence looming beside me stole my focus. Without even turning around, I knew it was Cash and my heart started beating faster, but I played it off well while Noelle cheesed like a fool.

"Can I help you, sir?" I asked, tilting my head to look up into his face. Just like in the room, he had that same amused look, like he knew I was undressing him with my eyes. Shit, as sexy as he was, I was sure he was used to bitches throwing themselves at him on a regular basis.

"Apparently, my ole lady thinks I should apologize for being rude." Shrugging, he nodded behind me, and I turned to see Ms. Banks in the waiting area motioning for him to do what she said. "See what I mean?"

"Yep, she don't seem like she playin' either, so you better get to it," I joked, and we shared an awkward laugh. I hated how fast my attitude toward him had changed, but it wasn't like I could treat him any kind of way here at work anyway.

"Yeah, she definitely don't fuck around."

That sexy ass smile was back, and I discreetly braced myself against the desk as I took him in. Before, his looks had stolen my attention, but now I had the opportunity to truly look him over. The white Givenchy t-shirt he wore hugged his upper body and arms in a way that showcased the work he had to be putting in at the gym. His light-washed Akiri jeans matched perfectly with the high top Jordan's on his feet and weren't too loose or too tight, which was sexy as hell to me. I hated a nigga in skinny jeans and I hated it even more when a nigga's pants were drooping off their asses like a soggy diaper.

"So, since I'm not tryna leave you with a bad impression, why don't you put yo' number in my phone so I can take you out to dinner." His phone was already poised and ready in his hand and butterflies instantly fluttered in my belly.

"Umm—"

"It's 773-654-1234!" My eyes bucked as Noelle jumped in, rattling off my number for me. Cash wasn't the first nigga that asked me out at work and just like every other time, I was going to deny him in the name of workplace etiquette, but that heffa just had to open her mouth.

"I appreciate you, friend." He flashed her a charming smile before quickly saving my number, and her crazy ass had the nerve to blush. "See, that wasn't so hard, now was it? I'ma call you later tho' so we can figure out where we goin' to eat." My mouth opened and closed ready to shut him down, but he had already swaggered back over to his grandma, who waved goodbye to me. *Cocky ass nigga!*

CHAPTER THREE
DINERO

I watched my little brother check his phone for the tenth time in thirty minutes and chuckled. No doubt it was a new woman that had his ass stalking his phone even as we sat counting the money our traps had made this week. I could see it on his face that he was growing frustrated by not hearing from whoever it was, and that made the shit even more funny. As Banks' boys, we were both blessed with our father's good looks and arrogant demeanor, which we witnessed our whole lives. Cash just happened to be the brother that had it the worst, so if a female wasn't getting back to him as fast as he thought she should, then the nigga was probably boiling on the inside. Being the big brother I was, I had no problem making it worse.

"Don't be over there fuckin' up the count while you stalkin', muhfucka," I teased, and he looked up with his face twisted in a scowl.

"Ain't nobody stalkin', nigga, I was just checking the time."

"Yeah, ayite. Granny already told me how thirsty you was being at her doctor's appointment, ole Rico suave ass nigga."

The way his mouth fell open after finding out our grandma had blasted him was hilarious. He knew her ass couldn't hold water.

"Dorothea need to chill! I ain't never been thirsty!" he grumbled, snatching up another stack of money. "She was the one being thirsty, talkin' 'bout how cute our kids would be and shit. Bro, I can't believe her petty ass. Next time, you better take her or have Pops do the shit."

"You bet not let Granny send yo' ass off, nigga. You already got one crazy baby mama, you definitely don't need another one." Even though the conversation was light, I was dead ass serious. That nigga's first baby mama, Vernique, was enough trouble all by her ghetto ass self.

"Naaaah, shorty ain't shit like Nique. She all about her business, she bad as hell, and her body! Nigga, shorty had ass for days!" he said, leaning back in his seat like ole girl had his mind blown, and I couldn't do shit but shake my head.

"You soundin' real thirsty, my boy. Yo' ass better grab one of them Dasanis before you die of dehydration in this muhfucka."

"You got me fucked up, nigga, I just told yo' ass—" he started, but his phone chiming stole his attention and he hurriedly snatched it up. Judging from the way his face lit up, I knew it had to be the shorty he was waiting on. I just tuned his caking ass out and continued counting the pile of money in front of us. It wasn't much left anyway, so I let him make it, and by the time he got off the phone, I was finished and already loading it back into the duffle bag.

"You cool puttin' that shit in the safe? I'm tryna catch shorty before she change her mind about letting me slide through." He reached for his keys and paused like I wasn't already holding the bag.

"Man, gon' head, ole parched ass nigga," I teased as he

sped off grumbling under his breath. He didn't even know, but I wasn't going to let his bitch ass live this shit down. I finished packing up and tucked my gun before leaving and locking our bachelor pad up.

Once I finally dropped the money off and headed home, I was tired as hell. Being a young rich nigga and part heir to the Banks empire had my days filled with making money moves. I barely ever had time to just rest, because money was the motive in all aspects of my life. That shit had been instilled in us since we were old enough to count by the great Kendrick "Dolla" Banks himself. Our pops was the man to see if you wanted to get in the drug game and he had the streets on lock until he handed the reigns over to me and Cash. Now we were the head niggas in charge and with his guidance, we were making millions, both legal and illegal. Between the drug money, our luxury car lots, the funeral home, and rental properties, we'd more than surpassed his expectations and I relished in his approval. Ever since I was a little nigga, I'd looked up to my pops and wanted nothing more than to be just like him. He was cool as hell, but deadly when the situation called for it, rich, and he'd snatched up the baddest female in the game. Now his ass was retired and able to enjoy the fruits of his labor with the same woman he'd come up with. He and our OG were always jet setting to somewhere that required a passport and blowing bags like it wasn't shit. Over the years I'd watched him spoil our mother like a true queen, and he made sure to let us know it was because she deserved it. I admired their love just as much as I did their wealth but had yet to find my own ride or die. Truthfully, I felt like they didn't make women like my mama anymore and the chances of me finding one of my own was slim to none. I'd only had two women to even come close to getting wifed up and they'd both fallen short of my expectations. The first being Tania, my high school sweetheart and the epitome of a good girl. Her father was a local minister and tried to keep a tight leash on her, but she couldn't resist a handsome ass bad boy, and the feeling was mutual. I loved how innocent she was and knew without a doubt that she was going to be my wife. That was until she got pregnant and allowed the good minister to force her into an abortion. At the time we were both seventeen and even though our shit wasn't ideal, I was willing to marry her and give her and our child the life they deserved. Somehow, she let her father convince her that me and the baby would ruin her life, so she got rid of it and then left the city to go to school. Last I heard, she'd gone to Berkeley on a full-ride scholarship.

After that, I didn't mess with women the same way. I was just fucking with them for a nut and nothing more, until I met Asha. Shorty was everything; beautiful, smart, ambitious, and the sex was explosive. She was the type of woman that could've taken me to the next level when it came to investments and smart money moves, being that she worked in real estate. That's actually how we met, she'd been the one who helped me with our rental properties, and that had been the reason we ultimately fell apart. After Tania, I learned to keep my lifestyle to myself unless necessary, so by the time I met Asha, all I allowed her to know was that I was a trust fund kid looking to invest in real estate. The first time she found out that wasn't true, we were involved in a shoot-out that had her packing her bags and leaving my ass high and dry. She did eventually let me know she couldn't fuck with me if I was involved in illegal shit and she stuck to her word. It had been over a year since I'd seen or heard from her and although I was disappointed, I knew she'd done the best thing for her and I couldn't be mad about that. After being left by the two women I deemed worthy of carrying my last name, over my occupation, I was resigned to never having what my parents did.

Honestly, I'd rather be alone than settle for some money hungry bitch anyway.

My stomach rumbled, reminding me that I hadn't eaten since earlier that day, so I took a quick detour and hit up the closest Harold's. As soon as I pulled up in my custom-painted, emerald green Camaro, all eyes were on me, but I was used to it by now. Everybody knew the infamous Banks boys, and if they didn't then they wanted to after seeing the amount of money we flexed on the regular.

Stepping out, I nodded to a few niggas that shouted what's up and then blew out an exasperated breath at the sight of Walt's ass just chilling on the side of the building. I was surprised he hadn't rushed me with how much he'd been blowing my phone up to get a meeting with me, but once I stepped inside the restaurant I knew exactly why. The same fine ass girl that had come on the block arguing with him stood at the counter in a pair of skintight jeans that had me wanting to squeeze her plump ass. I eyed her as she leaned over talking to the cashier and couldn't help fantasizing about how good she'd look bent over in front of me butt naked. Part of the reason I'd been so pissed about that bullshit with her and Walt was because I couldn't understand how his lame ass had even gotten with her in the first place, let alone had her acting a fool over him. Then again, I didn't know her from a can of paint, so her popping up on the block with that nigga's kid holding a vibrator with all that rah-rah shit could've been the way she got down all the time. As fine as she was, one thing I didn't fuck with was a ratchet ass female, so with that thought in mind, I averted my eyes and ordered my food.

Once the cashier gave me my receipt, I went to stand against the far wall to put some space between me and ole girl, but I could feel her eyes on me as I buried my face in my phone. While I waited, I checked a few emails and the social media pages for the car lots since people were always hitting us up on there. I was in the middle of writing a reply to an inquiry when a bunch of yelling from outside the restaurant snatched my attention, and there shorty and Walt were tussling on the sidewalk. Shaking my head, I went to finish what I was doing, but the girl called out my order number, stopping me. The scent of the gyro burger and fries with mild sauce had my stomach growling even harder, and I couldn't wait to get home and devour that shit. If I was being honest, it probably wouldn't even make it to my crib since it smelled so good.

With my food in hand, I planned to mind my business and walk right past the fighting couple, but when I got out there it was obvious that Walt had the upper hand. He had shorty pressed up against the building trying to choke her out, while the other niggas just stood there watching, instantly pissing me off. I wasn't usually a super save-a-hoe ass nigga, but I also wasn't cool with a man putting his hands on a female like that.

Using my free hand, I pulled my gun and pressed it against the back of his head, causing everybody out there to run off in a panic. "Let her the fuck go!" I ordered through clenched teeth, and he immediately released his hold on her, lifting both his hands in the air. As soon as she was free, she bent over, gulping in as much air as she could, while Walt pled his case.

"Aye chill, D, it ain't what you thinkin', man! This just a lil' disagreement between me and my lady!"

"You a lyin' ass bitch! You just flattened my fuckin' tires!" shorty yelled, pointing off to the side where a black Impala was parked with a back tire that was damn near on its rim. "And you made me drop my food too, ugggghhh!"

"Damn Ca'Mahri, stop! Get this bitch up off me, bro!" I'd only taken my eyes off the two of them for a split second, but that was all she needed to start right back attacking his ass. Now it was obvious to me that he'd been sitting out there waiting to see her reaction to what he'd done to her car, and my face balled up as I looked between him and her car in disgust. It was definitely some bitch nigga shit he was on to flatten her tires, then to turn around and choke her after doing it. Naw, he deserved the ass whooping she was laying on him, and I let her get a few more licks off before putting my gun away.

"Ayite, that's enough," I ordered, grabbing her arm midswing and pulling her back.

"Naw, fuck that!" She tried without luck to get out of my grip and run back over to him, but one look from me and she knocked it off, opting to fold her arms with a pout.

"Now do you have a spare?"

"I do, but it won't help none 'cause his goofy ass flattened both my back tires!" She scoffed, rolling her eyes, and I just dropped my head. I had planned on making that nigga fix her shit, but he was obviously more of a bitch than I'd originally thought. If it wasn't for the possibility of the police being called, I would've let her go finish him off, plus I'd already wasted much longer than I expected on their bullshit. At the very least, I could get shorty's car towed and wait with her until a ride came so she wouldn't fuck around and get killed or locked up messing with his ass. I shot a deadly mug over at that nigga as he struggled to get up off the ground and put in a call to my cousin Lou. After investing in his shop, he always made himself available to me, and I knew he'd get there faster than AAA would. "Who'd you just call?" she questioned, narrowing her eyes up at me in suspicion, and I had to stop myself from treating her ass. My fucking food was getting cold in my hands messing around with her, and she acting like I was the nigga who'd been choking her ass out a few minutes ago.

Sighing, I ran a hand down my face and said, "A tow truck.

You got somebody you can call to come get you?" Her face immediately fell and she blew out an irritated breath.

"My sister been MIA for the last hour, but I guess I can just schedule an Uber." She shrugged, pulling her phone from her pocket.

"Aye Dinero, bro, I—" Walt had finally picked himself up off the ground and had stumbled over to us.

"Get yo' ass the fuck from round here, nigga," I spat, freezing him mid-step. Knowing better than to come any closer, he stood there giving shorty an evil glare. "Yo, don't look at her, muhfucka! Do what I said!" I started in his direction, reaching for my gun, and he finally got the hint then stormed off angrily just as Lou's truck pulled up.

"What up, cuz?"

"Ain't shit, I need you to get this muhfucka to the shop for me and get her a couple tires put on," I told him, shaking his hand while he eyed Ca'Mahri behind me, and for some reason, that shit had me irritated. "Nigga, focus!"

"Shiiiit, how nigga? Lil' mama bad as hell! That's you?" He raised his eyebrows, cheesing, and I moved to block his view.

"Maaaan, get her ass some tires, you know I got you." I pressed a couple bills into his palm, knowing that it was more than enough to cover the favor, but whenever I used his services I always broke him off extra for the inconvenience.

"Guess that answers my question. You know I got you tho', cuz," he grumbled, counting through the five hundred dollars I just gave him before walking off to load up her car. With him taken care of, I turned back to Ca'Mahri. Her pretty ass was staring down at her phone with her nose turned up, not even looking like she'd just been fighting. I could definitely see why my cousin could barely take his eyes off her, with her smooth brown sugar skin, dark slanted eyes, and thick pouty lips. She had that natural type of beauty that didn't need any enhancements. Even her hair wasn't too high maintenance, sitting in a puffy ball on top of her head.

"Look, I appreciate your help, but you don't gotta wait with me. My Uber will be here in a half hour, so I'll just wait inside since I gotta order me some more food anyway." Shrugging, she stuffed her hands into the pockets of her hoodie and turned to go back into the restaurant, but for some reason, I stopped her. It was probably the same reason I'd stuck around this long and as much as my interest in shorty irritated me, I couldn't just walk away.

"Cancel the ride. I ain't tryna leave you out here alone while you wait, and I ain't sitting out here thirty minutes either so I might as well just drive you myself."

"But—"

"Cancel the ride and grab me another gyro burger while you at it," I cut her off, holding out a fifty-dollar bill to her. The look on her face told me she wanted to argue but knew better by now. "Come on, give me yo' keys so I can give them to my cousin, and make sure you get lemon pepper and mild sauce on my fries." I was glad that besides sucking her teeth she didn't put up a fight and just did what I asked. Rubbing a hand down my waves, I tossed my food in the nearest trash can and watched her switch back into the restaurant with my eyes glued to her ass. Just that fast, my plans of eating and taking my ass to sleep had gone down the drain.

CHAPTER FOUR

CASH

I woke up to Camille fumbling around the room and frowned at the fact that it wasn't even seven in the morning. I thought for sure the way I'd put it down would have her ass out until at least noon, then I'd feed her and fuck again before we went our separate ways. Obviously, she had some other shit in mind though. I watched with a smirk as she gathered her clothes and chastised herself before alerting her that I was awake.

"So, you was just gon' use me for some dick then dip out on a nigga? I don't know if I should be offended or impressed," I teased. The sound of my voice had her freezing up mid-reach, which gave me a perfect view of the pink thong her ass was swallowing up. I'd seen every inch of her body the night before, but somehow the sunlight had that shit hitting different, and my dick instantly started to wake up.

"Ahem." She cleared her throat and turned to face me with reddened cheeks. "I uh—I forgot I have an appointment, sooo." Her voice trailed off as she looked around uncomfortably.

"Or you really ain't have no business comin' to the hotel

with this nigga on some hoe shit?" I sat up, mocking what I'd overheard her saying to herself when she thought I was still asleep, and she narrowed her eyes at me.

"First of all, it's rude to eavesdrop and secondly, I didn't say hoe shit. I said hot girl summer shit." Instantly, the attitude she kept in her back pocket came out and she was rolling her neck at me. The way she'd switched that shit up only had my grin growing wider. "Seeeee," she dragged, clearly growing more irritated. Smacking her lips, she went to put on her clothes and I hopped up to stop her. It probably sounded crazy, but I wasn't trying to see her ass go just yet. I reached her right as she pulled her leggings up, which left her in only her bra. Gently grabbing her elbow before she could put on her shirt, I tried to keep my eyes on her face as memories of sucking her titties took over.

"Why don't you chill with me for a lil' bit. Let a nigga feed you or somethin'." I licked my lips and gave her my most charming smile, hoping she'd take me up on my offer as she eyed me suspiciously. "Look, you might as well, I know you hungry and bouta go eat anyway. At least if I take you it won't cost you nothin' but your time."

"Ha, my time is very much valuable," was her reply as she crossed her arms and shifted her weight to one leg.

"Shiiiit, mine is too, but I feel like you're worth it." A nigga was laying down his topnotch game and she was still looking at me like I wasn't shit. I couldn't even believe I was out here begging a shorty to spend some time with my ass. For sure, if Dinero got wind of this shit, he'd never let me live it down.

"Ummmm, maybe next time," she finally said, and I hid my disappointment with a nod.

"Ayite, cool." I was playing the shit cool, but I was salty as fuck. Any other female would've jumped at the chance to share a meal with a nigga like me. I knew bitches that would've been hopping on one leg and barking like a dog if I told them to, and here I was damn near begging Camille's ass to take her out. *Can't even be a fuckin' gentleman*, I thought, letting whatever she was saying hit my back as I made my way into the bathroom and shut the door behind me.

By the time I relieved myself and handled my hygiene, shorty was gone and forgotten about. The one time I tried to be on some stand-up shit and not just stick and dip, the roles had been reversed on my ass. I couldn't even trip, though, because at least I got some good pussy out the deal.

After quickly getting dressed, I left the hotel, squinting as the sun's brightness damn near blinded me. It was the time of year when the seasons were switching shit up so you never knew what you were getting when you stepped outside. Yesterday had been cold and today it was feeling like spring was supposed to, with birds chirping and shit.

I waited until I was sitting in the driver's seat of my Range, before powering my phone on and immediately, it was going off with multiple missed calls and texts. Besides a few of my slides, Vernique had been the main person hitting my line, but I already knew her ass wasn't up yet for me to see what she wanted, so I went under Dinero's contact instead. He'd called me twice and even though it couldn't have been an emergency, I still wanted to touch bases with him.

"Ohh shit! I know this can't be Cash up before lunch! Hell must have froze over!" his ugly ass cracked as soon as the call connected.

"Shut yo' lame ass up! Everybody ain't on that prison schedule yo' ass on!" I grunted, pulling out of my parking spot. For years my brother was up at dawn, doing some rigorous ass workout like he was training for the Olympics or some shit. He used to try and get me to join him, but I appreciated the fact that my metabolism was good, and the most I'd do was maybe hit the gym occasionally. "Fuck you call me for anyway, muscle head ass nigga?"

"Damn, you hostile as fuck this mornin'. Shorty stood you up or somethin'?"

My face instantly balled up at the suggestion. "Stand me up? Boy, you crazy as hell, you already know I sealed the deal on that!"

"Then the pussy must've been trash, ole' cry baby ass nigga." He was full of jokes today and I wasn't in the mood to play on the phone with his ass. Maybe it was because I was still pissed about how shit went down with Camille, or maybe it was too early, but instead of listening to him cackling like a bitch in my ear, I hung up, only to receive a text a second later.

Bro: Call me back when you get yo' thong out yo' ass, ole pussy ass boy!

I didn't even bother to message him back, I just put my shit on DND. *Hoe ass!*

After stopping through a McDonald's, I made the hour drive out to our family's estate in Winnekta. Our pops had bought up a whole block out there and had each home built from the ground up, with a huge wrought-iron gate around the entire property. It was straight boss shit, perfectly tailored to all of our likings, secured like Fort Knox, and secluded as hell. Dinero and I both had apartments in the city for nights we didn't feel like making the drive home, plus our bachelor spot that we used when we weren't trying to pay for a hotel, but he used that shit more than I did. I loved my nine-thousand-square-foot crib and preferred to stay there more than anywhere else. As soon as I stepped foot through the door, my maid Maria popped out asking if I was hungry and shit, but I just waved her off and headed straight to bed.

I don't know how long I slept before she was waking me up

with Vernique right on her heels. "I told you I could get him!" she shouted, pushing past Maria to come stand over me.

"Señor Cash, I told her to wait at the door like you instructed, but she forced her way in."

"And that's the problem, miss girl. I don't need to wait at no door. I got his son, so I can come and go as I please!" Vernique's expression was smug as she pointed at our son, Kash.

"Stop all that fuckin' yellin' while you holding him, bro, fuck wrong with you!" I snapped, wiping my eyes as I swung my legs over the side of the bed. I fucking hated that my OG had given this dizzy ass broad access to our homes on the strength of her grandbaby. It had her feeling bold and thinking she could come whenever she wanted and talk to our staff crazy. She only did the shit at me and my parents' cribs because she knew better than to go to Dinero's with that crazy shit.

Shaking my head, I checked the time and saw it was just after noon, which was probably why Kash was knocked out, drooling on his mama's shoulder. Simple bitch had dragged him over to my house during his nap on some thirsty shit. I was low key jealous his little ass managed to sleep while she was being all loud.

"It's cool, Maria, I got it."

"Yeah, gone head on, he got it!" Vernique mocked, adding some sauce to it. I knew Maria probably wanted to punch her in her shit, but she wisely went ahead and left quietly. "You fuckin' that bitch?" she asked, narrowing her eyes as soon as we were alone.

"What the fuck you want, Nique?" I intentionally avoided her question because there had been occasions when Maria sucked me up, but mostly because it wasn't none of her business. Vernique and I hadn't been fucking with each other for long when she popped up pregnant, but after I couldn't convince her to get an abortion, I tried to make it work. The problem was she wasn't wifey or mother material so that shit was short lived. I hadn't even fucked her in over a year, so it didn't make sense for her to be questioning me. At least I could say I didn't have an ugly baby mama, she looked just like Light-skin Keisha with the body to match. Unfortunately, though, besides birthing my heir, that was all she had going for herself.

"Ewww, check yo' tone, baby daddy." She sucked her teeth and moved around me to lay Kash down in my bed. After making a face that resembled mine when irritated, my little man quickly relaxed into my memory foam pillow. "I need you to keep Kash for me." She cocked her head up at me and put her hands on her hips.

"That's all yo' ass wanted?" I frowned.

"Well, yeah." A stupid look covered her face as she hunched her shoulders. She'd blown my phone up and came disrupting my sleep just to drop him off, when she could've just given him to Maria at the door. I had to walk the fuck off before my hands found themselves around her neck, but she followed right behind me and stood at the bathroom door while I brushed my teeth.

"You know I got my lil' dude, I'll just drop him back off on Monday." Presuming the conversation was over, I rinsed my mouth and grabbed my Listerine, only for her ass to still be standing there. I eyed her as I swished it around in my mouth, noting the same goofy look on her face.

"Actually, it's gonna be longer than the weekend." This time she winced as she spoke, and I already knew some bullshit was coming. I definitely didn't mind keeping my son, but with all of the shit me and my brother had our hands in, I couldn't have him as often as I wanted. When I was too busy, my parents would pick up my slack and even Dinero chipped in when he could, but they were still on vacation for another few weeks. I tried to prepare myself for whatever she was going to come out of her face with next. If she needed me to keep him an extra week, I could probably handle that, I'd just need to move some shit around, but considering that she was unemployed, she'd better have a good ass excuse.

"How long you talkin'?"

"I don't know and it shouldn't matter anyway!" she exploded, making my jaw clench. "I have him twenty-four-seven and he's your son too, nigga! It ain't fair you get to live your life like a fuckin' bachelor while I'm out here lookin' like a single mother and shit! I'm goin' to Cancun for spring break with Ne'veah and nem, so it should be two weeks but if it's longer, then hey, it's just gone be longer." By now Kash was sitting up, probably unable to continue his nap with all the yelling she was doing and lucky for her, his eyes were right on us. As bad as I wanted to, I'd never spazz on her in front of him, so instead of going back and forth with her dizzy ass, I swallowed my anger and managed to just give a stiff nod. Plus, I couldn't lie, she had been the one doing most of the work when it came to him, and I'd rather her leave him with me than to just drop him off with a random relative.

"Ayite, but—"

"Thanks, baby daddy!" she gushed, cutting me off before darting out of the room without even looking our son's way. I couldn't even do shit but let out a deep sigh after taking my second L of the day. *Damn, City Girls up two and it's only the fuckin' afternoon.*

CHAPTER FIVE
CAMILLE

"Where the fuck were you last night?" was the first thing out of Ca'Mahri's mouth when I answered my phone. The question immediately had me thinking about Cash's tongue and the way he'd expertly delivered the dick. It had been everything I imagined it would be and after I got home I'd slept like a baby, only just now powering up my phone and returning calls. Stretching, I let out a long moan and winced at the soreness I felt between my legs. It had been a few months since I'd let a nigga get close to the pussy, and even longer since a nigga had done it so well that I was feeling it the next day. Cash had definitely stamped his name in it, which was why I had to move around instead of taking him up on his offer. Every nigga I'd ever messed with that fucked that good came with a bunch of toxic bullshit. Baby mamas, community dick, toxic masculinity, and a propensity to lie always went hand in hand with good dick, and I just knew Cash had some or all of those traits, which meant I couldn't fuck with him.

"Hello, hellloooo! Did this bitch hang up on me?" My

sister's voice snapped me back into the present and I had to laugh.

"Ain't nobody hung up on yo' slow ass."

"Oh, 'cause I was bouta say!"

"Nothin', you was just gon' call me back!" I said smugly, already knowing that's what she'd do.

"And would! Now where was you last night, hoe? I needed yo' ass and you was MIA." Without even seeing her face, I knew her spoiled ass was pouting.

"What you mean you needed me? What happened?"

"Walt's stupid ass is what happened. I stopped at Harold's last night after work and this goofy ass nigga saw me and slashed my damn tires! Ole bum ass!" she grumbled, and I immediately caught an attitude. I couldn't stand Walt from the moment my sister first brought him around. Call it intuition or whatever, but he just looked like he was full of shit and after the months she'd invested in him, he proved me right! It only took me a couple of times to get played with by a nigga and I learned my lesson and could see a lame a mile away. Unfortunately, my sister was a true romantic and was the blinded by love type. Being the big sister I was, I tried to put her up on game, but she never listened and always ended up having to call me so we could bust a nigga or a bitch head. Since Walt got saved the last time, he obviously thought shit was sweet enough to come back and try my sister, but I definitely wasn't going to let the shit slide.

"Oh, I know you fuckin' lyin'! Where you at right now? I'm gon' tase the fuck out his ass!" I hopped up, completely forgetting about how sore I was, so I could grab my keys.

"Nope! He tried to choke me out and everything, but it's cool. That same fine ass nigga from last time just happened to be out there and he saved the day once again. Got my car towed and everything. I'm waiting on him now so he can take me to pick it up from his cousin's shop, since I couldn't reach yo' ass last night," she said smartly while I tried to register everything she'd just told me. I knew exactly who she was talking about because I'd peeped his fine ass too, I was just wondering why he'd been comfortable enough to pay for her tires. In my opinion, chivalry was dead, and niggas these days weren't going out of their way to pay for shit without getting something in return. I didn't like that she was technically indebted to him and I really didn't like that he knew where she lived.

"Why the hell you let him know your address? You don't know that nigga from a can of paint! What if he kidnap you or something?"

"Yeah, ayite! I'll fuck his fine ass up! Plus, he look too good to be out here kidnapping bitches," she defended, sounding naïve as hell.

"Well, turn on your location then so I can at least know where you at just in case."

"Fine, *Mama*!" she spat sarcastically, and I could hear the grin in her voice. "He just pulled up so I'll call you back—"

"Tuh, hell no! Stay on the phone 'til you get in the car so I can let him know how I don't play about you!" It was crazy how hard I was going over her and this stranger when I'd literally spent the night with a nigga I didn't know, but as hard as Ca'Mahri pretended to be, she was marshmallow soft in real life. She took more after our mama and only popped off when she was pushed to her limit, while I took after our daddy and was a firecracker at all times.

"Girl, you really be taking this big sister thing too far for real," she groaned, and I could hear her getting inside his car and his deep ass voice in the background. "Here, my sister wants to talk to you." She sounded like a little ass kid pouting, but that didn't bother me at all. As soon as his voice came on the line, I jumped right into protective big sister mode.

"I just want you to know that it's war behind my sister so make sure you return her in the same condition that you picked her up in or me and you gone have a problem!" I let him know matter of factly, only for his ass to bust out laughing.

"Oh, you the one that came out on the block with her acting all wild and shit, huh?"

"Yep, and will do it again too, so take heed." Even as I gave the warning, something about his voice had somewhat put me at ease.

"You got that. I don't want no smoke with you, big sis. Ca'Mahri in good hands, though, I'm gon' return her in perfect condition," he promised, and I had to admit that he seemed cool. Before I knew it, my sister had gotten back on and rushed me off the phone. A second later, I was notified that she'd sent her location, and I relaxed a little more. Since Ca'Mahri's bald-headed ass seemed to be okay, I checked my other missed calls and messages but there wasn't anybody I wanted to get back to at the moment, so I just scrolled social media. It was my day off anyway and I didn't have shit planned unless Ca'Mahri or Noelle wanted to go out later.

After a few minutes, my mind drifted to Cash and I wondered if he was on Facebook or the gram. He didn't give off the vibe of a nigga who was constantly posting, if he even had a page, but I couldn't help myself. *Just looking can't hurt*, I thought as I typed in his name with a K first, but none of the pictures were his. The normal spelling ended up being the right one and his fine ass popped right up, sitting in a Rolls Royce with thick knots of money in his lap. Of course, his conceited ass had a picture like that. It was just further proof that he was exactly the type of nigga I should stay away from, but that didn't stop me from continuing to snoop. I didn't even know what I was looking for, or why I was looking after only a one-night stand. Then again, I knew exactly what I was trying to find out. I wanted to find reasons why I made the right decision by leaving him where he was at. I'd been hyping myself up before, but the truth was, I was slightly regretting not staying when he asked. At the very least I could've gotten in another round to hold me over until I found someone worthy of sharing my cookies with. The way my taste was set up, though, it wasn't likely going to happen, so I'd just let the opportunity slip through my fingers.

"Aha! I knew this nigga had some kids somewhere!" I hissed, sitting up abruptly to get a closer look at the picture of him and an adorable baby boy. The kid couldn't have been much older than five months and since the picture was from a little over a year ago, he was probably going on two by now. A child that young definitely had a mama somewhere with her feelings still involved. I could only imagine the type of baby mama drama he would bring my way, especially if he was still fucking her, like most niggas in his situation. Somehow, even after going in prepared for the worst, I was still feeling salty about being proven right. Like I was legit mad that I'd even allowed myself a second to reconsider my stance on niggas like him, when I knew better. The craziest part of the whole thing was that we'd only had two interactions, one of which was a damn sneaky link! Shaking my head, I went and exited out of the app before I could piss myself off any further, just as a notification came in that Ca'Mahri had arrived at her location. After a quick check, I was glad to see that she was at an actual mechanic shop and it wasn't too far away from where I lived. At least it seemed like dude was on the up and up, besides the fact that I had been so busy threatening him I didn't get his damn name. Unbothered by how much I may have been annoying her, I texted my sister and asked for his name. The bubbles indicating she was replying popped up, as I made my way to the kitchen to get my salad out of the fridge. I'd been planning on saving it for lunch the next day, but since I wasn't in the mood for cooking it was going to get demolished sooner. I quickly dressed it with some ranch and dug in while watching my phone and a few seconds later, she sent an eyeroll emoji and what I assumed was his name, which was Dinero. I instantly turned my nose up and hoped that his mama hadn't been that ghetto to name him that shit, but I knew it was a big chance she had. A giggle bubbled in my throat thinking of how similar his and Cash's names were, when I damn near spit out the food I was chewing. With the quickness, I went back to his page and confirmed that it was the same nigga my sister was with on his profile picture. The caption further proved how small the world was because right there in black and white were the words *brothers*. It figured Dinero and Cash were brothers, and that just made me even more worried about Ca'Mahri's naïve ass. I was poised to send her a text warning her when a call from Noelle stopped me.

"Hey girl."

"Soooo, tell me. How was it? Where did he take you? Did you have fun?" she asked like she could barely contain her excitement, and I rolled my eyes. I'd forgotten all about me telling her I was meeting up with Cash. There hadn't been any dinner, though, unless she counted the way he'd feasted on me, and the only fun was the multiple orgasms I'd had.

"We, uh, we didn't go to dinner, we went to The Four Seasons." My voice turned high-pitched and trailed off, making her gasp.

"Ooooh, you hoe! Talking all that shit and you let him talk you out the panties," she said smartly. "Quiet as kept, I was hoping you'd let him knock the dust off that lil' pussy.... thot ass could've got dinner first though."

"Ha, ha, real funny, hoe, but ain't nobody talked me out my damn draws, I talked his fine ass out of his!" Cash had been the one trying to stick to his word and take me out. Except the moment he pulled up in a midnight blue Wraith looking like he'd just stepped off the block, I wasn't even hungry anymore, not for food anyway.

I shuddered just thinking about the way he'd puffed his blunt and eyed me from head to toe lustfully while considering my suggestion of skipping dinner. That along with the length of time it'd been since I got some dick sealed the deal for me. I thought I'd be okay to just get some and be on my way just like any other time, but the dick Cash delivered had me shook and after seeing that the nigga had a baby, I understood why.

"Okay, well, I need details now! Was it big? Of course, it was big, that nigga walk and talk like he got a python! Straight BDE! I just need to know if you plan on doing it again, and if he got a brother! Hell, I'll take the daddy or an uncle at this point 'cause I know it run in the family!" she cackled, and I had to laugh right along with her crazy ass.

"Nah uh, you might as well calm down. I have no intentions on seeing his ass again so it won't be no relative for you, baby girl."

"I know you fuckin' lyin'! Why would you cut off a nigga that beat the pussy up just to go back to your dry spell?"

"First of all, I never said he beat shit up. You just assumed—"

"So, the dick was trash?" she cut me off condescendingly, shutting my ass right up, before continuing when I still hadn't said anything. "Mmmhmm, exactly, try that shit with somebody else. Now why you not tryna see my friend no more?"

"That nigga got a whole baby mama and you know how I feel about that shit, with yo' friendly ass," I said, and she quickly sucked her teeth. Just like Ca'Mahri, Noelle was well aware of my long list of rules and thought they were stupid.

"Here you go with this shit again! Girl, nine times out of ten, a nigga gon' have a baby mama or two tucked off somewhere, it's how he deals with her ass that matters. You ain't even gave him a chance yet and you're already tryna throw him away," she preached as I picked at my salad and sighed. She'd made a good point, but in my experience, niggas didn't know how to keep their baby mamas in their place, and it was easier to just avoid the headache all together than to deal with the drama that came along with those types of situations. I could already see myself getting hurt again, and I honestly didn't know if I would be able to handle another nigga disappointing me. I'd fuck around and stab a motherfucker this time around, so it was best if I just kept things on a sexual level, especially if kids were involved.

"I'd rather be by my damn self than to lower my standards just to keep a man around. Didn't I just tell you what the fuck Walt did to Ca'Mahri? Ain't no nigga bouta have me out here looking crazy behind his baby mama, I don't care how good the dick is!" I huffed with my face scrunched up. Cash wasn't about to have me fighting bitches or worse, getting pregnant and stuck with his ass for the next eighteen years and beyond. Nope, wouldn't be me! The sex was definitely good, but it wasn't worth all that, not from him and nobody else.

"Don't yell at me with yo' mad ass, I'm just speaking facts. You can keep yo' lil' perfect man checklist, but what you gone do when he bring his grandma back up to the hospital?" she wanted to know, sounding amused as hell like she was getting front row seats to my dysfunctional ass life.

"You already know I'm gon' keep it professional as always," I explained with a shrug, knowing it wasn't going to be that simple. There was no telling what type of energy he'd have for me the next time we saw each other. It damn sure wasn't going to be with open arms after the way I shot his ass down at the hotel. I could see it in his face that his pride was hurt, and fucking with a nigga's pride could make them disrespectful as hell. And just as disrespectful as he could get, I could get on that same shit too. I just hoped it wasn't at my job.

CHAPTER SIX
DINERO

As soon as I stepped inside my parents' house, I could hear them laughing while some Jodeci played over their home audio system, and I couldn't do shit but shake my head at their old freaky asses. If it wasn't for their maid letting me know they were in the kitchen, I would've turned my ass right back around. My parents were overly affectionate, and the shit had only gotten worse since we'd gotten older, and I damn sure wasn't trying to walk in on them in a compromising position. I rounded the corner to the spacious kitchen with my hand covering my eyes just in case.

"Nigga, you better announce yourself when you come up in here!" my pops said loudly, causing my mama to giggle. "You was 'bout ready to see some grown man business goin' on if you would've been a few minutes slower."

"Kendrick, leave my baby alone! You can uncover your eyes, Dinero, yo' daddy just messing with you!" My grown ass peeked first like I was eight years old again and was glad to see that they were hugged up in one chair with their robes on before I fully removed my hand.

"You wrong for that, old man," I grumbled, dropping down into one of the empty chairs at the table and helping myself to the spread they had laid out. No doubt Gina, their personal chef, had gone all out for their return. There was fruit salad, muffins, pancakes, waffles, cheese eggs, bacon, sausage, and ham. It was enough to feed an army, but I knew my pops could run through half that shit by himself. The nigga had always been huge, weighing over three hundred pounds and standing at six four. I was glad I'd come when I did or else it wouldn't have been enough left over for me.

"Old? Who you callin' old? Keep playing, I'll make yo' ass another little brother!" He squeezed my mama tightly and winked at me with a slick grin.

"I don't know who the hell you gon' be doing that with 'cause this factory has been shut down for about twenty-seven years." My mama shot him a serious look even though her tone said she was playing.

"Broooo, I ain't tryna hear about y'all asses making babies. I'm tryna eat!" I complained around a mouthful of food. It was bad enough growing up with them being all over each other, but as an adult it hit different. I would've thought their old asses would have chilled by now, but they continuously let us know they were still getting it in.

"Boy, this my damn house, don't be comin' up in here tryna bust up our groove, like you and yo' brother ain't out there fuckin' everything movin'!"

"What she said," my pops instantly co-signed, giving her a kiss on the cheek.

"What she say? Yooooo, put on some clothes, man! Fuck y'all old freaky asses on!" Cash entered the kitchen with his face balled up as my nephew trailed behind him.

"Why don't both y'all niggas take yo' asses home! You lucky we ain't walkin' round this bitch naked!"

"Stop it, Kendrick, he got Money with him." My mama slapped his arm before wiggling away at the sight of Kash, who she'd affectionately dubbed Money. In full grandma mode, she was up and tightening up the same robe my pops had just yelled at Cash about, before scooping up the toddler. I'd seen first hand just how true it was that grandparents were easier on their grandkids than they were their own kids. Kash's little ass was bad as hell and fucking with my mama, he got away with half the shit he did. She attributed everything to him being a baby and she bought his ass whatever he wanted. The little nigga had every toy you could imagine, clothes and shoes that weren't even out yet, and his jewelry was damn near shitting on mine because of her. I was sure if we left it up to him, he'd never leave his grandma's house just because of how much she spoiled him.

"Vee didn't call and tell me she was sending him over. How long do you have him for?" my mama asked as she kissed his chubby cheeks repeatedly. Cash had already made himself at home and was piling a plate with a little bit of everything on the table.

"Shiiit, I don't know. The hoe—I mean Vee dropped him off the other day talking bout she going on vacation."

The room fell silent as all eyes landed on him. I even went to touch that nigga forehead because he was sounding way too calm to have let his baby mama just drop his shorty off and not know when she was coming back.

"Nigga, what the fuck you doin'?" he fussed, slapping my hand away roughly.

"Shit, I'm tryna see if yo' ass sick or something."

"How a bitch without a job go on vacation? I know you ain't payin' for that shit?" My pops was looking even more confused than me. As much as he loved Kash, he'd be the first to admit that he hated Vernique being the mother. In fact, he'd been ready to kill her ass along with me and Cash when we found out about her being pregnant, but my mama had convinced him not to, thankfully.

"Hell nah! Ain't shit comin' out my pocket unless it's for Kash Banks! Maybe her thot ass got a sugar daddy or somethin'." He shrugged, continuing to shove more food into his mouth. "I ain't trippin', long as she brings her ass back." Me and my pops shared a look at his nonchalance but dropped the conversation. As much as we talked shit about her, Vernique wasn't a terrible mother, so I wasn't totally against her having some time to herself. I just hoped she brought her ass back like he said, because the lifestyle Cash lived was far from suitable to raise a toddler.

"Well, I'm just glad he's going to stay awhile. Matter fact, he can stay the night with us," my mama said, causing Pops to groan. She ignored his displeasure as she carried an excited Kash over to an empty chair and loaded him up a plate.

"Damn, baby, we just got back and ain't even got settled in yet. Stop acting like you ain't just see his lil' ass before we left!" She stopped mid-scoop and shot him a menacing glare that shut down any argument. Kash was definitely spending the night.

"Good, now that that's all settled." My brother clasped his hands together and turned to me with a grin. "We got some shit we gotta handle anyway." Just from the look on his face, I knew he'd been banking on our mama volunteering to keep his son and I was already shaking my head.

"Slick ass nigga. What type of shit you talkin' 'bout?" I questioned, already suspicious of what he'd be getting me into that night.

"It's some money moves. Just trust me, bro." He grinned, once again further proving that he was on some other shit, and even though I knew it, I still agreed, hoping that whatever it was he had me tagging along for wasn't a waste of my time.

* * *

Hours later, we sat parked outside of a ranch-style home on the west side. It had been a half hour since we'd pulled up and the nigga still hadn't said what we were doing there. I could surmise from the all black he wore and the sawed-off rifle in his lap that somebody was about to get fucked up, but that was about it.

"Nigga, you gone tell me what the fuck we doin' here or what?" I finally questioned, growing more irritated by the second.

"You already know what I'm on," was his vague ass reply, but just when I was about to ask him to elaborate, a hooded figure stepped out onto the porch and he sat up in his seat. Without speaking, he reached for the door, cuffing his gun at the same time, and was out of the car fast as hell. I'd barely had a chance to step off the curb and he was already across the street hemming the dude up.

"L-look, Cash, I'll g-get your money. I swear—I'm in the middle of a deal!" the man shrieked as Cash shoved the barrel deeper into his neck.

"I look like I give a fuck about a deal when yo' ass already owe me? You got me out here searching for yo' ass like I'm a feign or some shit. Nigga, run me my money!" Visibly shaken, dude stuffed his hand down into his pockets and produced a bunch of crumpled bills, but it was too dark for me to make out how much it was.

"T-this is all I got!" By now he had tears streaming down his face as Cash released him long enough to snatch the money from his fist. It took him no time to count it out and when he did, his face grew tighter than it already was.

"What the fuck is this shit!"

"It-it's all I got!" Now fuming, Cash shoved the money in his pocket and brought his gun back up, this time aiming it at his temple.

"Naw, I think you can get more. So I'm gonna suggest you take yo' ass back in the house and come back out with the $450 yo' ass owe or yo' shit gone get splattered right here in front of yo' mama crib!" Immediately, my head snapped in that nigga's direction at the cause for all of this shit. A funky ass five hundred dollars was why he'd pulled me away from my plans of getting some sleep. I wanted to crack his ass in the back of his head for wasting my damn time. We made way too much money to be hounding niggas for that measly shit.

"Aye Roy, you good over there?" a voice called out, snatching me from my thoughts. Without hesitation, I pulled my nine from my hip and pointed at the approaching figure.

"Nope, and you ain't either now, with yo' nosy ass," I said evenly, causing him to stop in his tracks and throw his hands up. Looking between me, Cash, and his homie, he obviously decided he didn't want any parts and took off running in the opposite direction. *Pussy ass nigga!*

"Now, where were we? Ah, that's right, you was bouta go get my money up out yo' people's crib." Shock and then worry quickly flashed across Roy's face when my brother released him and nodded toward the house he'd just come out of. He stalled for a hot second then sped away, and I turned my heated glare onto Cash. "Ahhhh, that nigga scary as hell!" He cracked up laughing as he watched dude rush inside.

"Bro, I know damn well you ain't got me out here over no funky ass $500. The fuck he owe you for anyway?"

"His ass bet against Brick City, knowing them boys got the

game on lock, goofy ass nigga. I been waiting to catch up to his ass, he lucky I ain't just pull up dumping." Disdain was written all over his face and I couldn't do shit but shake my head at his childish ass. If it wasn't for the fact that dude might try some funny shit when he came back, I would've left him standing right there by his damn self. Thankfully, that wasn't the case, though, because about five minutes later, Roy returned with more money and a dainty gold necklace that no doubt belonged to a woman.

"I look like a pawn shop, nigga? What the fuck I'm s'posed to do with that?" Cash huffed, looking at Roy's open palms like he had a handful of shit.

"That's all I could get from the house, Cash, man! I swear, that necklace gotta be worth at least two fifty; it's the only real jewelry my OG got. You could at least give it to yo' girl or something." By now I was tired of both their asses and ready to go.

"Maaaaan, get the fuck on!" I watched as my brother snatched everything up and sent Roy's ass scrambling away. "Come on, bro." He casually tucked the shit in his pocket and prepared to go back to the car, while I looked on in disbelief.

"Nigga, yo' ass crazy as hell! How you just made that man steal from his own mama and shit?" I asked, falling into step beside him.

"So, fuck Roy and his mama. He's lucky I ain't fuck his goofy ass up for even wasting my time with this shit, talkin' 'bout give it to my girl!" He turned his nose up like the thought alone disgusted him before his brows lifted. "Low key, I might fuck around and give it to Ma though."

"Yo' ass bet not give that shit to my mama, muhfucka! If Kendrick don't fuck you up for giving her that gold-plated shit then I will!" And I meant that! If I thought I saw it mixed in with our OG's jewelry, I was beating his ass and snitching so he'd get it twice. Shock covered his face and he instantly came to a halt in the middle of the street.

"You think this shit fake for real?" Just that quick he was prepared to go after that nigga, but I quickly pulled him back.

"That's what the fuck you get, bring yo' ass on!" I ordered, pushing him toward the car before he had me out there any longer with that bullshit. With him now on the passenger side I jumped behind the wheel, ignoring his complaining as I pulled off. Despite getting us out of the situation, I knew Cash was going to be looking for a whole other set of problems with Roy if he found out the necklace was fake like I suspected it was. I just hoped the nigga had enough sense to get out of dodge, because my brother was just petty enough to beat his ass over that little bit of money.

CHAPTER SEVEN
CA'MAHRI

It had been a long week and I was finally off after endless call lights, irritating nurses, lazy CNAs and a few short-staffed shifts. I prided myself on working in the nursing field just like my mama and sister, but there were days that I never wanted to return to the Buckingham Pavilion Nursing Center for real. Having to coexist with racist residents and bitches who came to work with attitudes would have the most professional women ready to act a fool, but for the most part I kept it together and was able to finish my shifts without incident. Cam and Noelle just didn't know how good they had it being able to work together. I didn't fuck with none of the bitches at my job, and since my mama and I worked different shifts, I only ever saw her when she was punching in and I was leaving for the night. That's why I was so glad to finally be leaving and not returning for two whole days. As soon as I dropped into the driver's seat, my phone was ringing with a call from my sister.

"Heeeeeey, biiiitch!" her and Noelle slurred as soon as I answered, making me chuckle. Since they had both been off they begged me to call out of work so we could day drink, but I'd declined. I may have disliked my job, but I didn't play when it came to my money. Obviously, they'd gone without me though.

"Y'all petty! How I'm just now getting off and y'all hoes already drunk?" I teased, finally pulling out of the parking lot and into traffic.

"We told you to call off! You're the one tryna be topflight CNA of the world and shit!" Noelle's reference to the movie *Friday After Next* had them cackling like fools as if she'd said the funniest joke in the world, so I knew they were tore the fuck up.

"Couldn't be me, 'cause I would've called sounding like I was dying!" Camille added, quickly putting on her fake sick voice. "I'm sorry (cough, cough). I can't make it today, my temp is 105 and I feel lightheaded every time I stand up." Once again, they fell into a fit of giggles while I rolled my eyes at them. My sister could talk all she wanted, but she called off even less than me. If it would've been the other way around, she definitely would have gone in just like I did, so I wasn't putting much into her little drunk jokes. Noelle, on the other hand, called off for anything. I'd seen the girl call out sick because of a headache and then spend the day shopping.

"Anyway, we know yo' ass done clocked out now, so you might as well go change and then meet us over here." I was already shaking my head. After the eight hours I'd just put in, the last thing I wanted to do was get cleaned up only to go back outside. The way my body was feeling, I'd fuck around and fall straight to sleep after my shower.

"Hell naw! I'm taking my ass to bed if I go home—"

"Ha! I knew yo' lame ass was gone say that shit and that's why we're already over here."

"Ughhhh, bitch, I'm taking my key back," I groaned, even

though I was lying. Camille and I had always been close and had even lived together for a while when I first moved out, so her not having full access to my apartment wouldn't even feel right. And the bitch knew it too.

"Yeah, yeah, just hurry up and get here!" she said before hanging up on me.

It took me no time to get to my apartment and it felt like my tiredness immediately went away. I gathered my nursing bag that I always carried and climbed out, ignoring the people that were standing around kicking it. Since it was the weekend, my city was even more live than usual and I'd seen a bunch of people out on my way there. I'd barely made it up the walkway and I could already hear the loud ass Meg Thee Stallion blasting from my stereo system. Both Camille and Noelle were in the living room flexing how strong their knees were as they rapped along to the lyrics of "Thot Shit," and I wasted no time pulling my phone out and joining them.

"Okay, let me gon' head and quit." I stood up out of breath and watched the video before sharing it to my Snapchat. The niggas were definitely going to go crazy, because we'd fucked it up for real.

"See, I got Meg knees, I can go all night!" Camille bragged, dropping down and twerking some more while Noelle, who seemed just as tired as me, egged her on.

"Yesssss, bitch, fuck it up!"

Camille's ass and the way she moved was putting even the baddest stripper to shame and even though we'd both gotten blessed with our mother's shape, she clearly knew how to work it better than I ever did. We geeked her up for a few more minutes before she finally stood with a triumphant grin. "You know what? We should go to the club for real. I feel like shakin' somethin'."

"Oooh, we should!" Noelle agreed breathlessly before

turning to me with her eyebrows raised in expectation. "You down?"

"Hell yeah! Let me go get ready right quick." They both agreed and headed out to Camille's to get dressed since she lived close to me. I knew exactly what I was going to wear and since my hair was already done in a high ponytail that I'd accomplished with the help of YouTube university, all I'd need to do was shower.

An hour later, I was dressed and ready to go. I'd put on a gold, silky button up and left it open with a thin, black belt, some black, satin booty shorts, and some sheer, black knee highs that had a bunch of runs in them. On my feet, I wore a pair of gold heels that had a thick strap around the ankle, and I pulled everything together with gold hoops, a layered neck-lace, and my favorite Michael Kors watch. My face was beat lightly and I'd added some clear Fenty lip gloss to make it pop. Nobody could tell me I wasn't a baddie with a fatty, and I couldn't wait to get to Club Indigo so I could show off.

After making sure I had everything, I drove to Camille's to pick her and Noelle up but before I could even park, they were strutting out of her door. They were both looking good as hell and I rolled down the window to let them know it.

"Daaaaaamn, y'all fine as hell!" I shouted, making Camille flip her hair and put on her best model walk and Noelle strike a pose. Noelle was wearing a blush-colored, spaghetti-strapped bodysuit with a pair of black distressed jeans that had tears all the way down the front and back, giving the world a peek of her luscious skin underneath, and matching black pumps. Camille had on a white corset top that cut low and crossed over her chest, with a pair of high-waisted black shorts, a black blazer, and some pointy-toed heels. Just like me, they hadn't done too much with makeup and only wore lip gloss and lashes.

"Ooooh, you look cute!" Camille squealed, tossing her thirty-inch Brazilian hair over her shoulder once she got in the car.

"Yess, you're giving very much sexy rockstar bitch!"

"Ayeee, just a slight flex, y'all already know we're bouta have all them bitches mad tonight!" I predicted. It never failed, whenever we all went out together, hoes were always hating on how effortlessly we snatched niggas' attention. Most of the time they left us alone, though, and only talked shit from a distance, but there had been a few we had to check both verbally and physically.

Camille sucked her teeth with a flick of her wrist. "They're always mad, but I ain't in the mood for that bullshit tonight. I'm just tryna get drunk and shake my ass."

"Period! Cam's ass don't need no more stress anyway," Noelle chimed, making my brows dip in confusion, but before I could even ask what she meant, Camille shot her a nasty look and cut up the radio. I was going to let her make it for the moment, but I put it in my mental rolodex to ask her ass about it later. The rest of the ride was silent besides the King Von that was blasting through my speakers.

Thankfully, by the time we got there the line wasn't as long as I'd expected, and we got right in. The place was wall-to-wall packed and I could instantly feel the jealous eyes of some of the women and the lustful glares of the niggas as we walked through and made our way to the bar.

"First round on me!" Noelle let us know before squeezing through the only open spot and motioning for the bartender. I swayed while I waited and sang along to Summer Walker as I took in my surroundings. There were a few sexy niggas also standing around the bar waiting to get their orders taken, and I slightly nodded in approval, even though I knew I wasn't going to speak to any of them. After Walt, a bitch needed a breather, especially since the nigga I wanted hadn't shown any interest in me and probably never would. Both times we were in each other's space Walt had me showing my ass, and just from our interactions, I could tell he wasn't into a bunch of rah-rah shit. I was honestly surprised he even went out of his way to help me because he always seemed like he had more important things to do. Then when he picked me up to get my car he was completely different, friendly even, so I just knew he'd want to keep in touch. His ass fooled me, though, because as soon as Lou dropped my keys in my hand, he got ghost. My ego was bruised as fuck after that, but I just went ahead and put him and our interaction behind me.

"Ugh, who is that?" Camille questioned, pointing at a girl who was sitting on the other side of the bar staring a hole in the side of my face. Instead of looking away, she continued to gawk at me once our eyes locked.

"Tuh, hell if I know, but she can definitely catch these hands and feet!" By now the girl's friend had joined in on the staring contest with just as much contempt, and I found myself grimacing. I didn't know either of them from a can of paint and yet they were mugging me like I'd fucked their man on their birthday.

"See, I knew it was gone be some bullshit. Next time we go out, we're going somewhere else." Camille was already wrapping a hair tie around her bundles even as she complained. I wasn't trying to ruin our night with bullshit, though, and as long as they continued to just look then I'd remain cool.

"It's okay, Cam, let them hoes stare. I'm good as long as they stay over there with that miserable shit," I huffed just as Noelle turned around and handed us each a double shot of Patrón.

"Who staring?" Her head was already swiveling to look for whoever wanted an issue.

"Nobody," I said, throwing back my shot, and was immediately ready for another. "We s'posed to be getting fucked up and twerking on our hot girl shit, y'all."

"Was it these funny lookin' bitches walking over here?" she asked, ignoring me and turning up her nose in the direction those bitches had been in.

"Yep, that's them."

I spun around to see that both girls were now making their way over to us, and my eyes rolled up into my head. Even when I tried being on some chill shit it seemed like drama followed me. Taking a deep breath, I told myself I'd try to defuse the situation first and if that didn't work, I'd just have to do what needed to be done. The closer they got, though, the more familiar the first girl became, and I realized it was Walt's damn baby mama that had come to my house. A second later, they stopped in front of us and just stood there looking stupid for a second before the friend finally spoke up.

"You mess with Walt, right?" she asked stupidly, sending us into a fit of laughter. They both looked way too old to be asking questions they already knew the answer to. Before when she brought her ass to my house, I'd been too pissed to pay her appearance any attention, but now that my head was clear, I was wondering how I'd even fucked with a nigga who would go up in her raw. Her face was riddled with so much acne sis looked like a Hershey cookie and cream bar, same color and everything, then she had nerve to have makeup caked over the shit. Everything about her said low budget, from her lifting and crusted wig down to the too little ass heels she wore. It had to be her ass because I knew first hand it wasn't her face, shorty was a tip drill if I never saw one!

"I been done with that nigga, girl, he's all yours." I chuckled, speaking directly to the baby mama whose face balled up, making her even more ugly than before.

"Bitch, he been mine! I'm his baby mama, he ain't ever leaving me alone!"

"Or me!" the other girl added, sounding dumber than the first.

"Hold up, *this* the baby mama?" Camille moved closer, pointing a finger in her face.

"We sure are, and—"

"Ohhh, I been meaning to catch up with yo' ass! This must be my lucky day, I get a two-for-one special!" Camille instantly went for the girl's wig and at the same time, I swung on the mouthy one. She was clearly all talk, because just like a bitch who couldn't fight, her arms were flailing aimlessly. Now I was mad that she'd even wasted my time. Grabbing ahold of her long knotless braids, I held her steady and went to work on her face while Noelle bounced around with her phone out, occasionally throwing in punches of her own. I was still swinging when I felt myself being lifted into the air and felt a hard body pressed against my back.

"You won, bruh, let shorty go." Despite it having been a week since I'd heard his voice, I knew immediately who it was talking to me and a chill traveled down my spine.

CHAPTER EIGHT
DINERO

Ca'Mahri's body stilled in my arms, but she kept her tight grip on ole girl's hair. I'd been watching her since the moment she and her girls hit the bar, so as soon as shit looked like it was about to get crazy, I made my way down. Unfortunately, I wasn't fast enough because by the time I got to them, it had already turned into a whole damn brawl. Since Cash had brought his nosy ass down with me, he'd taken it upon himself to snatch up who I assumed was her sister, and she was giving him a hard time too. The other girl with them stood off to the side, looking between me and Cash, stunned.

"Let me go!" Ca'Mahri squirmed, trying her hardest to get out of my hold while still keeping a tight grasp on shorty. "Noelle, come get this nigga off me!"

Noelle's eyes bucked and she immediately shook her head. "Bitch, is you crazy? I can't do nothin' with that big ass nigga!"

"Scary ass hoe!"

I bit back a chuckle from how feisty her little ass was, even when she knew she had no wins in the situation. Even if I didn't exactly approve of it, I had to admit that she was consistent and for some reason, I liked that about her. I considered just walking off, but as stubborn as Ca'Mahri had proven to be, I knew she'd just drag that hoe right along with us. Glancing over, Cash had managed to get the women separated and was now just wrestling around with Camille, while the other girl was laid out on the ground. We literally had the attention of the entire damn club by now, though, and I was getting irritated. "Man, let her go!" This time I put a little more bass in my voice with the order.

"Nope, she shouldn't have been runnin' her mouth!" Ca'Mahri grunted, landing another blow on shorty's head that had her wailing loudly. I guess that was the final straw for her, though, because she turned and yanked away, leaving more than a few braids behind. The ass whooping Ca'Mahri laid on her had her ass gathering her friend and getting the fuck out of dodge. This ignorant ass girl was yelling after them and swinging the missing braids around her head. I lowered her feet back to the floor but kept a firm hold on her waist, so she wouldn't try to chase behind those bitches. "Uh, can you let me go now?" she huffed, craning her neck to glare at me, but I ignored her little attitude and nodded for the security that was approaching to keep it moving.

"Nope. Yo' ass clearly need a babysitter 'cause you stay in some shit," I half joked. Ca'Mahri was the definition of not judging a book by its cover, because her sweet face would fool anybody when she was really a whole beast on the inside. That wild shit wasn't something I was normally attracted to, but I had to admit, she intrigued the fuck out of me. As hard as I'd tried, I couldn't get her fine ass off my mind the past week, and I'd hoped some pussy would help, but it did little to nothing. Having her this close now only reminded me that it wasn't shit like the real thing.

"I don't need nothin' from you! Matter fact, where'd that brute take my fuckin' sister? I just wanna get her and Noelle and we'll leave." She tried to sound calm, but I could feel her literally shaking and I didn't know if it was because of the fight or the fact that I hadn't let her go yet, but I wasn't letting her out of my sight either way. With the ratchet shit over, everybody had moved on to what they'd been doing before, and I noticed that Noelle, despite looking fearful, had eased her way over to us.

"She's fine. My brother took her up to our section, we can go get her *together* though." I emphasized the word and damn near laughed at the way her nose turned up. Shorty was hell, but I wasn't that bitch ass nigga Walt, and I didn't need to lay hands on her to have my way. All it took was a stern look and just like before, she piped down and allowed me to guide us toward the section with Noelle following behind closely.

Surprisingly, when we hit the landing we were met with Cash and Camille pressed up against the balcony, looking as if they were in a heated discussion, and every woman that had been up there was gone. He had her trapped between him and the railing with an arm on either side and his head tucked down so that he was speaking directly in her ear. Knowing my brother, he was trying to lay his game down on her, and I didn't blame him. Camille was just as beautiful as her sister, so it was only right that he try to get in where he fit in.

"Oh, yo' brother got her alright! He over there molesting her damn ear! Get him off her!" Ca'Mahri started going off and the commotion had the two separating. While Camille seemed irritated, Cash rubbed his jaw with a sneaky grin, completely unfazed by our presence.

"I'm cool, y'all. Let's get up outta here," she sighed, folding her arms and moving further away from my brother.

"Damn, you ain't gone introduce me to yo' people?" he questioned, clearly amused.

"And ain't! You ain't nobody they need to know!" They began going back and forth while me and Ca'Mahri watched in confusion. I was thinking Cash was trying to get at her this whole time, but it was obvious they already knew each other.

"Hold up. Cam, you know this nigga?" Ca'Mahri asked, stepping closer to them since I'd finally let her go.

"No!"

"Yeah!" they turned to her, answering at the same time, before Cash finally noticed Noelle standing next to me and grinned widely. "What's up, friend? Why yo' girl tryna act funny and shit?" He put her on the spot and all eyes quickly fell on her. Not knowing what to say, she shrugged, looking like a deer in headlights.

"Awww, y'all bitches keepin' secrets now?" Ca'Mahri fussed, crossing her arms and glaring between the two of them.

"Nuh uh. Don't look at me, that's Camille's business to tell."

"It's nothin' to tell. We met, we kicked it, and I ain't seen this nigga since," Camille filled in with a hump of her shoulders. Even I knew there was more to the story judging from her behavior and so did her sister, because Ca'Mahri already had her lips twisted in disbelief, but leave it to Cash to call her out though.

"You call all the nasty shit I did to you the other night kickin' it?" his crazy ass blasted, making her mouth fall open in shock. "Bro, this shorty who call I was waiting on," he continued to further prove his point, and I finally put two and two together. Since he hadn't brought the shit back up, I'd just assumed the pussy wasn't worth talking about, but now it was obvious that she wasn't fucking with him the way he was fucking with her.

"I can't believe yo' ass just said that."

"And I can't believe yo' ass tryna play like you don't know a nigga—matter fact, come holla at me." His ass didn't even give her a chance to agree before grabbing her by the elbow and leading her away, to which she didn't put up a fight.

"Nuh uh!" Ca'Mahri immediately tried to intervene, but I put a stop to that.

"She cool, man, come sit yo' hot ass down and have a drink or something." She looked like she wanted to go back and forth with me about it, but thankfully, Noelle was on my side.

"Yeah, let's do that, 'cause we already wasted enough time on the bullshit." She scoffed and headed right over to the table that held various bottles. Ca'Mahri cut her eyes at me next, but I just threw my hands up and followed her girl, copping a squat on the couch before preparing me a cup of Hennessey. I was hoping she'd do the same and not just up and leave since her attitude was all over her face. It took her a few seconds, but eventually she came over and sat down, making sure to scoot as far away from me as possible. I just shook my head and chuckled at her childishness. I understood she was probably still pissed about everything that had taken place, but I wasn't about to kiss her ass.

It wasn't long before she began to slowly lighten up enough to let Noelle mix her a drink and was even moving her body a little bit to the music. A few niggas from our crew eventually showed up, along with some other ladies. They all came over to greet me, and Russ, the only single one of the bunch, quickly snatched up Noelle, leaving her girl and me all alone.

"You good?" I asked, closing the space between us so I could pour more liquor in my cup. I'd been taking her in the entire time, enjoying every bit of her thick, silky-smooth legs and her sweet scent that seemed to keep creeping up my nostrils every time she moved. The way she tucked her head and looked over at me like she was trying to figure me out before she spoke was cute as fuck, but I was finding everything about her to be attractive to me.

"I'm cool, besides my people leavin' me to entertain some niggas," her smart ass said with a roll of her eyes. I had to laugh, because Noelle was tucked off in the corner with Russ and no doubt her sister and Cash had left the vicinity completely. I knew when his ass pulled her away that they probably weren't coming back, but I wasn't going to tell her that.

"They're chillin', besides, I know my company ain't *that* bad." I palmed my chest with my free hand, and leaned away like I was insulted, even though I knew her issue wasn't with me. She sighed and let out one of those girly ass giggles.

"I guess," she hummed. "At least you're being nice....kinda."

"Damn! What you mean? I'm always nice," I lied. I was well aware of how my demeanor could be perceived when I was dealing with anybody besides my family. My patience was set up different after my experience with Tania and Asha. I treated everybody like they could potentially be a threat, but I hadn't necessarily been that way with her. Despite my lack of friendliness during our past encounters, I had gone out of my way for her, which was some shit I normally wouldn't do.

Of course, she knew I was full of shit, though, because she puckered her lips to the side and pointed at them, basically letting me know she didn't believe me.

"That's fucked up. I left that much of a bad impression on you?"

"I meeeeean." Ca'Mahri shrugged, letting the word fade as she took a sip of her drink. Normally, that shit wouldn't have bothered me at all, because I wanted to seem unfriendly, I wanted muthafuckas to see me and walk the other way or not feel the need to converse. There was really only two reasons why I'd even be semi-approachable to somebody and those were business or sex. If you weren't trying to help me make money or slob me up, then I really didn't have shit for you, but hearing Ca'Mahri say it hit different. Suddenly, I felt the need to change her impression of me, since she wasn't aware of how nice I was actually being the few times we'd been around each other.

"Daaaaamn, I thought helping you out *was* me being nice." My brows dipped and I eased closer.

"Ha! If that's what you call nice then you gone need to work on that, my dude."

I feigned hurt while she busted out laughing, not realizing that she'd given me the perfect opportunity to try and spend time with her. Stroking my beard, I nodded. "Ayite, ayite. So, why don't you let me take you out and get some practice in." Even I had to admit that the shit was smooth, and had clearly flattered her judging by the way she'd grown silent as her lips spread into a grin.

"So, you want me to be yo' guinea pig?" Her eyes were full of amusement.

"I wouldn't say guinea pig, more like a crash test dummy," I cracked, making her head fall back in laughter, and as corny as it sounded, that shit was music to my ears. I could definitely fuck with hearing that shit every day.

"See, these drinks gotta be kickin' in for real," she said, shaking her head, even though she took another drink.

"Naw, I'm just charming than a muhfucka, but on some serious shit, let a nigga treat you. I'll even make reservations, so you know it's real. We already past the awkward shit and damn near a couple anyway. I done checked a nigga for you, maintenanced yo' car, and been to yo' crib before. Ain't shit left to do but break bread together." I already knew I was laying it on thick but when I wanted something, I got it, and Ca'Mahri would be no different.... At least I hoped anyway. She seemed like she was mulling the idea over in her mind, but since she hadn't come right out and said no, I knew I had her.

"I guess I can give you a chance," she said casually.

"See, that wasn't so hard, was it?" Lifting my cup, I waited until she brought hers up as well and we toasted. I was already thinking about getting some help from my OG, because there was no way I was trying to fuck this up.

CHAPTER NINE
CAMILLE

"Ooooh, fuck, Caaaaash!" I cried out and threw my head back as my legs shook uncontrollably. I'd tried to keep quiet, but he was sucking the soul out of my pussy! His ass knew it too, because every time I made a sound he let out a grunt in response. Somehow, a conversation with Cash had quickly turned into him talking me out of my shorts and burying his head between my legs. The nigga definitely had a silver tongue! He was so skilled I almost forgot why I was keeping my distance from his ass in the first place. Shit, I was ready to make an exception for him that I never would've made before with a lesser nigga, and that was crazy as hell. Which was why my ass was laid up between his seats with the console digging in my back as he devoured me like the finest meal he'd ever had.

"Yeah, let that nut go so you can hop on this dick." His voice came out husky and demanding, pushing me right over the edge.

"Hmmmm, I'm comin', shit!" I grabbed the back of his head, forcing more pressure on my clit before erupting all over his face. My legs immediately gave out and if he wasn't positioned the way he was, I surely would've landed right on my ass. He already had me on my second orgasm, and the mischievous look on his face let me know he was about to punish the fuck out of me. With an arm wrapped around my waist, he took his time lifting me up so I was straddling him and planted wet kisses all over my chest, while he released himself. "Don't, I'm not tryna go back in there smelling like pussy." I frowned. It was bad enough that the expensive ass cologne he was wearing would already be clinging to me, but I didn't want to face my sister and Noelle smelling like I'd let a nigga fuck me in his backseat.

"You goofy as hell, you think you goin' back in that bitch!" he said in between pecks, completely disregarding my request. I didn't know where the fuck he *thought* I was going, but it damn sure wasn't with him! I was prepared to go off on his ass, but truth be told, that shit was feeling too good mixed with the head of his dick between my slippery folds. Grabbing the sides of his face, I brought my lips to his and greedily accepted his tongue, growing even more excited from the taste of my juices. I could hear him tearing open a condom, and I lifted up just enough for him to ease it on without breaking our kiss. "Damn, your shit pouring! Got my hands slippin' off the rubber!" he huffed, looking between us like that would help.

"Hurry uuuuup!"

"I got this shit, girl, don't rush me!" It was a shame how bad I was feigning at this point. I reached to help him out because my pussy was thumping so hard, but his rude ass knocked my hand away. "Ayite, got it. And you better ride this big muhfucka like a big girl too! Don't be runnin'!" he warned, giving me a hard look as he placed himself right at my opening.

"I got this!" I threw his words right back at him and sassily rolled my neck. His ass must have forgotten how I'd had his ass moaning the last time, but I was more than ready to remind him. He snorted and hit me with smirk that I took as a challenge. Looking him dead in the eyes, I slowly eased down his length and had to bite my lip to keep from moaning as he filled me up.

"Come on, I thought yo' ass was bouta ride this muhfucka like a porn star! You lookin' like you gon' tap out and you ain't even started yet!" he huffed, smacking my meaty ass cheeks before roughly pulling me forward. The motion drove him deeper inside me and I yelped, unable to hold it in. It seemed like everything his ass did, turned me on to the max, so instead of complaining about how hard he'd hit my booty or the way he was tapping my uterus, I planted my hands on his shoulders and began winding my hips. "Fuuuck, girl! Just like that," he groaned, leaning his head back and staring up at me with partially closed lids. His hands roamed all over my body, either rubbing up and down my thighs, or squeezing my ass.

"Mmmm, *baby*!" With ease, he popped both of my titties out and gently bit down on one while pinching the other. It felt like he was everywhere all at once, causing me to go even harder. Our moans and the sound of my gushy pussy filled the truck, quickly rising over the low music he had playing. It was no doubt that anybody walking by knew what was going on, especially when he started fucking me back.

"Ohhh, I'm baby now, huh! Now you know who the fuck I am, right?" he taunted breathlessly, pulling my hair so my throat was left exposed. As bad as I wanted to be defiant and not answer his ass, my mouth fell open.

"Yesssss!"

"That's what I like to hear, baby, say that shit louder!" he barked, burying his face in my neck as he slid off the seat so he could be in full control. All I could do was hold on for dear life as he drill pumped into me faster and faster, and the familiar tightening in my stomach let me know I was about to explode.

"Fuck, fuck, YESSSS!" I screamed as an orgasm hit me so hard that tears slipped from my eyes.

"Damn, you so fuckin' fine." He looked up at me with his forehead scrunched, and I knew he was on the verge of filling the condom. "Fuck! I'm cummin'!" Groaning, he smashed his lips against mine.

His grip on me tightened as his dick throbbed and we stilled, both riding the wave of our orgasms. With ease, I could say that Cash fucked me better than any nigga ever had, and that was saying a lot. It was like he knew exactly what to do, and what not to do. Where to touch me and when. After only two encounters he had it down to a science that niggas I'd fucked with for months or years hadn't even grasped, and now I realized why I'd really been so mad about finding out he had a baby mama. I was dick dizzy. One session had me confused, but now after two, I knew for sure I was beyond gone. *What the fuck had I gotten myself into?*

* * *

The sun shining in my face woke me out of a very comfortable sleep and my eyes popped open. Déjà vu hit me hard and fast as I looked around and noticed the same hotel setup from the first time I'd linked with Cash, and I released a low groan. I couldn't even blame my backsliding on the alcohol either because I'd only had a shot, so fucking him in the car and then getting a room with him were both conscious decisions, unless I could count being a dizzy dora as an excuse.

"What the fuck, Camille!" I whispered to myself and glanced behind me to see if Cash was up. If he was still asleep I could try to sneak out the same way I had the last time, but luck wasn't on my side because as soon as I turned my head, I locked eyes with a very alert Cash.

"You still talkin' to yourself, huh?" he cracked with a raised brow. Rolling my eyes at the wide grin on his face, I tightened the sheet around my naked body and stood to my feet. It seemed like he was even more annoying during daylight hours, or maybe it was just my guilty conscious rearing its ugly head. As I moved about the room looking for my clothes, I could feel his eyes on me and I was almost positive he still had that same goofy ass grin on his face. "What you lookin' for, maybe I can help?" he finally said, and something in his voice had me snapping my neck in his direction.

With narrowed eyes, I looked him over and realized he was shirtless in only a pair of boxer briefs and socks with his arms casually tucked behind his head. "Nigga, where's my shit?"

The question had his smile widening and his eyes lit up in amusement. "If you talkin' bout yo' clothes and phone, they're somewhere safe, and I'll get 'em back to you after we eat and chill for a while." He shrugged just as a knock sounded at the door. His psycho ass took his time swinging his feet over the side of the bed and strolling past me to answer it. I was so stunned I couldn't even move let alone speak and could only watch him retrieve a bag of IHOP that he'd had delivered.

"Come on, Cash, stop playin'. I have work today," I whined, impressed with how fast I'd thought of the lie. By now he'd made it back to the bed and was already pulling out containers like I hadn't said shit at all. "Cash!"

"Yo' ass off the whole weekend, bruh, I already asked Noelle. Now do you like cheddar on yo' eggs? 'Cause I didn't order no other kind."

"Really nigga? Are you out yo' fuckin' mind?" I hissed, not even surprised at this point that he only stared at me blankly instead of answering. Deciding not to keep playing with him, I continued to look around the room for my things. Shit, I was willing to take his shit at that point, but there wasn't a stitch of clothes anywhere, not even in the drawers. "Ughhhh!" Finding nothing underneath the bed clear also had me groaning, and I slammed my fist down on the floor.

"Yo' food gone get cold you keep fuckin' around," Cash said matter of factly with a mouth full of pancakes. He was calm as hell, like he wasn't trying to hold me captive or something, and I felt my forehead crease as I looked at him. It really didn't make any sense for somebody so handsome to belong in a damn psych ward.

"Okay, so all I gotta do is eat and you gon' give me my shit back?"

"And chill." He shrugged before shoveling a forkful of eggs into his mouth.

"Fine." Sighing, I made my way back around to my side of the bed where my tray of food sat unopened with a bottle of orange juice. I hadn't even realized how hungry I was until I lifted the top and the smell of buttery pancakes slapped me in the face. Maybe it wasn't going to be so bad to hang out with him for a while. The nigga had gone out of his way to keep me there. And albeit crazy, I had to admit it was kind of sweet. Getting comfortable in bed, I dressed up my stack of pancakes with butter and syrup and added a little bit of salt to my eggs before I dug in. We ate together in silence for a few minutes and before I knew it, he was tossing his empty container back in the bag.

"You wanna pick the movie?" he asked, cutting on the TV to Netflix, and I grinned sneakily.

"Yep." Snatching the remote, I typed *Bridgerton* into the search box and started it on the first season. Since his ass wanted to play, I was going to bore him to death and get in some binging while I was at it. He seemed unmoved by my choice, though, but I figured it was just because he wasn't aware of what the show was about.

"Ain't season two out already?"

"Yeah, but—you watch this?" I was unable to hide my shock as he nodded, like it wasn't a big deal.

"My granny and OG was watchin' it one day when I was over there and I ended up gettin' into it on some high shit. I mean, it was ayite, so if you wanna start at season one I'm cool with it." Why did I instantly get that tingly feeling? I didn't know if it was because he hung out with his family, or because he actually liked the show, but either way, it had me seeing him a little different. I liked a nigga with layers, so knowing there was more to him than being rough around the edges and a baby daddy with good dick was....refreshing. Now I wanted to know even more about the man behind the arrogant bully I'd gotten used to.

Since I didn't want him to know that I'd only cut the show on to irritate him, I agreed to just watch from season one. I finished my food halfway through the first episode and tossed my trash before heading into the bathroom to handle my hygiene. It was cool to eat before brushing my teeth, but there was no way I could go any longer without taking care of that. I was pleased to see that Cash had already used one of the toothbrushes and hadn't just elected to spend the day with morning breath.

By the time I finished brushing and showering, episode two was coming on and Cash was under the covers looking comfortable as hell. He eyed me as I strolled back over to the bed clad in only the plush white robe the hotel had provided, and licked his lips sexily. My still wet Brazilian weave hung in curls down my back and although I was basically fresh faced, I knew I was looking good enough to eat. Tossing the covers back, he patted the empty spot beside him, and I climbed in, propping my pillows up behind my back, but he pulled me over to his side so that I was snuggled against his bare chest. The nigga smelled amazing, and I had to admit it felt good as hell pressed up against his warm body. He didn't even realize how hard he was making it for me to stop myself from getting attached. I was fighting an internal battle with myself on whether or not I should give him a chance to prove me wrong and unfortunately for me, my heart was winning out over my mind and common sense.

We ended up spending the entire morning and part of the afternoon there, alternating between watching TV, talking, and giving each other multiple orgasms. I found out how much he loved his family, and about his son and his relationship with his baby mama. It was easy to listen to him talk and it was even easier to open up to his ass too, and by the time we were checking out, he knew a lot more about me and my family. I even clued him in to my last relationship, which hadn't ended well, and was a big part of why I felt the need to vet any man I was interested in. That's how I knew shit was going downhill and fast. In a matter of half a day, I'd fucked around and got caught up.

CHAPTER TEN

CASH

I pulled into our family's car lot with a big ass grin on my face. Spending damn near a whole day with Camille had a nigga walking on cloud nine and I was already wanting to see her fine ass again, even though I'd just left her. After she shot me down that first time, I pushed her ass out of my mind. It wasn't hard either, because having a toddler around twenty-four-seven kept me busy as hell, in addition to my other obligations, but thinking about her and seeing her were two different things. I'd noticed her right before the fight broke out, and had already decided I was going to make my presence known at some point despite not liking how she'd handled me before. When I saw her slinging that bitch around the dance-floor, though, I headed straight downstairs behind Dinero's ass and snatched her up. She was just as surprised as I was to be running into each other and was giving me a hard time until I put some dick back in her life. I couldn't even front, though, Camille had that wet, wet. She had me addicted at this point, which was why I trapped her ass in the room with me. Wasn't no way I was letting her good pussy having ass dip on me again. I didn't give a fuck what she thought she was going to do. Her ass was stuck with me, whether she knew it or not.

"What's up, John Q?" Dinero's lame ass came swaggering into my office as soon as I sat down.

"Man, fuck you!" I grumbled, giving him the finger for added effect. With a wide grin, he took a seat across from me and shrugged, completely unbothered by my aggression.

"I'm just sayin', you're the one out here tryna steal hearts and shit, ole soft ass nigga." Shaking his head, he sat back and rubbed his hands together, clearly amused. "Wait til I tell Pops, the popcorn playa kidnappin' muhfuckas. Don't forget Granny called it," he made sure to point out.

"Yo' ass just hatin' 'cause her sister wasn't fuckin' with you like that! Get you some game and shake that hate off, that shit don't look good on you, my boy," I advised, balling up a piece of paper and throwing it at him. He swiftly knocked it right back, making it fly past my head and hit the wall behind me.

"Ahh, gotta be quicker than that, goofy! And fuck you mean, get some game? I got game, and I can get a woman to spend time with me without holdin' them hostage," he shot back, giving me a pointed look. "What did you do with shorty clothes and shit anyway?"

"Technically, I didn't hold shit. I just sent our clothes down to get washed and told them I'd call when I was ready for them to bring 'em back. By the time they did return them, though, Camille was bagged so she didn't even trip." When the maid knocked on the door with our clothes neatly folded and shit, she just looked at me and busted out laughing. She said she never would've thought that's where they were and that she figured I'd put them in the truck or something. That was where I'd put our phones though.

Shaking his head with a grin, Dinero reached over and slapped hands with me. "You're crazy as fuck, lil' bro, but as long as you got the desired results, I guess I can't trip. I'm damn sure gone be tellin' our grandkids about this shit tho', you can bet that!"

"Man, fuck outta here!" I smacked his hand away, and he fell out laughing like a whole fool. "Don't we got a couple pickups today? While you in here fuckin' with me and shit! Go make yo' self useful and get the cars ready or somethin'," I grumbled, shuffling around papers on my desk. Our luxury car lot was a front just like every other business, but we also transported there as well as the funeral home. Whenever we had a big drop, we made it our business to be in the building to make sure shit went smooth. Besides, the nigga Julez that was coming in that day was from Cali and was always trying to switch shit up at the last minute. If it wasn't for the fact that our pops fucked with his, then we wouldn't even continue making deals with his ass.

"Everything already set up, cry baby ass nigga. If you wasn't late you would've known that. Oh, I forgot, you was too busy tryna give a bitch Stockholm syndrome!" his smart ass said, finally standing up to leave. "The truck comin' in an hour. That nigga Julez was on bullshit and moved the time up again." Instantly, I grew pissed off. If I would've tried to stay at the room with Camille any longer, I would've fucked around and missed the whole damn drop because of his inconsistent ass!

"Bro, next time he pull that shit, we taxin' his ass, and I don't care what Pops say," I huffed, taking my eyes from my computer screen so he knew I was serious. It seemed like niggas only understood shit when you hit their pockets, and if that's what needed to be done for him to get his shit together, then so be it. Family friend of my pops or not.

I could already see the unease on Dinero's face, but he only nodded before ducking out the door. He'd always been the more diplomatic one when it came to how we ran shit, while I stayed ready to turn up on a bitch ass nigga regardless of the outcome. My pops always said that he'd somehow given Dinero more of his brains and me more of his brawn, because that nigga calculated the pros and cons of every situation. He was probably already trying to figure out a way to keep our business ties intact without ruffling any feathers, but I meant what I said. That nigga was going to come out of his pocket the next time or he was going to find a new connect.

Before I knew it, an hour had flown by and I stood outside with Dinero as the carrier trailer loaded up six of our cars and another one unloaded three. That was our method of exchanging drugs for money. We would load up a few cars with kilos of our product and send them off at the same time we'd have the customer stuff the money in the cars we were receiving. It was a perfect cover for what we really had going on, because wasn't no cop going out of their way to pull those cars down and search them. We'd been doing the shit for more than a year already and it was working like a charm.

"What's up, Banks and Banks?" Julez stepped out of the back of a Rolls Royce, dressed in a whole three-piece suit. He always called us that lame shit and every time I wanted to knock the smirk off his face.

"Same shit, different drop." Dinero shrugged, handing the paperwork for the cars over to the driver before dapping Julez up. He tried to stretch the same hand out to me and I just looked at it like he had shit all over it.

"Nigga, shit ain't gravy! Next time yo' ass switch the schedule, I'm either dockin' your load or chargin' you extra!" I sneered, daring him to say something slick so I could beat his ass. The grin on his face faltered, and he looked over at Dinero. "Fuck you lookin' at him for? He already know what's up!"

"Aye chill, Cash." My brother quickly jumped into mediator mode, but I wasn't trying to hear shit he was saying.

"Yooooo, you funny as fuck." He chuckled, looking back and forth between us before shaking his head in disbelief. "You can't tax me, nigga, the price already set along with the weight, unless I want more. Do you need me to call y'all's old man to explain this shit to you again or somethin'?"

"I don't give a fuck what deal my pops made with yours! *We* supply *you*, so whatever we say goes, muhfucka, and like I said, next time you gettin' docked or taxed!" I stepped forward, even more amped up than before, but Dinero lifted his arm between us in an effort to hold me back.

"Aye D, man, I'm bouta get up outta here. Talk to this nigga or somethin'," his bitch ass huffed and stormed back over to his car.

"What the fuck, Cash? You need to keep yo' attitude in check, nigga! Who cares if he changes the time, he's still our biggest customer and you bouta put his money in somebody else pockets with this macho shit!"

"You sound like a bitch! Why I gotta check my shit, but y'all lettin' that nigga walk around thinkin' he can do whatever he want? I bet every car on this lot his ass gone come with some more bullshit next month, then what, you gon' let that shit slide again!" I spat. I loved my brother and I could even appreciate his mellow nature, but even I knew if you gave a nigga an inch they'd take a mile.

"Man, you trippin', take yo' cranky ass home or somethin'," was his reply, only irritating me more because he hadn't answered my question. Waving him off, I strolled over to my truck and pulled away. I honestly didn't have a problem taking the rest of the day off and leaving his ass to handle the cars and the money.

As bad as I wanted to actually go home and sleep, I pulled

up to our parents' crib so I could grab Kash. I hadn't taken him to do anything fun since I'd gotten him, mostly because he'd been spending all his time with my mama and Maria. The little bit of time I did have him was either early in the morning or right before he went to bed, but even I knew that wasn't enough. Parking right out front in their circular driveway, I let myself in as usual and I could already hear his little bad ass running around while my mama yelled for him to stop. His little footsteps got closer and a second later, he was whipping around the corner, damn near slipping on their recently waxed floors.

"Daddy!" he shouted as soon as I picked him up. My little man was cute as hell, walking around with my whole face on his miniature body. He even had my attitude and bossy nature. My mama swore he was just a worse version of me and that it wasn't just a case of the terrible twos, but I was hoping he'd grow out of it after his birthday, to be honest.

"You up in here givin' my mama a hard time, lil' nigga!" I asked, tossing his little bad ass in the air a couple of times, making him giggle uncontrollably before I put him over my shoulder.

"Nooooo!"

"Noooo? It don't sound like it! It sound like you need to be beat up, 'cause you know I don't play about my OG!" I threw a couple of soft jabs into his side and his chubby ass laughed until he snorted.

"Noooo! Graaaaaanny!"

Right on cue, my mama came from around the same corner ready to plead a case for him, but once she saw me she visibly relaxed. "Boy, I thought something was wrong!" she fussed, throwing her hands on her hips.

"He-he try to beat me up!" Kash called himself snitching,

and I threw another punch. He was kicking and squirming in an effort to get down now that my mama was there.

"You bet not, Cash. I'm gone beat yo' ass if you don't put him down." Just like he knew she would, she was there to save the day, and when I acted as if I still wasn't going to do what she said, she started toward me with her face screwed up.

"Ayite, ayite! Damn!" Flipping him over, I put him down and as soon as his feet hit the floor he was off again, probably on his way to fuck with my pops.

"What yo' ass want? Comin' over here botherin' my baby!" She was already on her way back to where she'd come from, and I followed behind her until we reached the kitchen where she had a ton of shit stacked up on the counters and table.

"I came to get him since y'all won't barely let his bad ass come home," I teased, and she just smacked her lips and waved me off before lifting up a wine glass and taking a sip.

"Whatever you say, Cash, you know you love being able to come and go as you please."

"I'd be able to do that if he stayed at the crib with me too."

"Oh, 'cause yo' lil' in-house hoe would keep him?" she said dryly, talking about Maria. For whatever reason, she hated that girl with a passion and always had something slick to say whenever she was brought up.

"I'm not fuckin' with you, Ma. What's all this shit in here anyway? It looks like y'all need to hire Maria. What you do, fire yo' staff?"

"Tuh! I wish the fuck I would! Hoe ain't bouta be in here tryna throw that tired pussy at my husband!" She rolled her eyes. "But if you must know, I'm preparing some stuff to donate. The closets are next and if you and your brother have some things you want to get rid of, bring them over here too." I was still stuck on her thinking anybody besides her would try to get with that old ass nigga, but I was going to skate right past that shit.

"I got you, but let me catch up with Kash ass, though, before it gets too late."

"Okay, just make sure if you're bringing something to have it here by Friday," she let me know before I ducked out of the kitchen. Since I didn't hear Kash running around anymore I figured he was somewhere doing some bad shit, because it was never good when that nigga was quiet. I'd already gotten yelled at, though, so I wasn't going to even bother with him. Instead, I headed toward my pops's office, and that's where I found him sitting on the old man's desk and eating a big ass Blow Pop.

"Not you givin' him candy on yo' one-of-a-kind African Blackwood?" I had to fuck with him because he would've never let me or Dinero anywhere near that shit when we were younger. His ass always tried to pretend like he wasn't going soft for that little nigga, but Kash clearly had both his grandparents wrapped around his sticky little fingers.

"Mind yo' business, Money knows how he's supposed to treat quality shit. Ain't that right, man?" he asked, and Kash nodded like he was paying attention to anything other than the big red sucker in his hands. "See? Now I heard about what happened today at the car lot." He quickly switched the conversation, looking up at me solemnly, and I already knew some bullshit was coming.

"Why y'all steady comin' down on me like that nigga ain't violating every time he do that fluky shit?" I frowned, feeling myself about to get pissed all over again. Of course, Julez had gone and ran his mouth like a little bitch, unless it was Dinero who'd told him, which would've been even worse.

"Trust me, I made sure that Grayson got on Julez about his

part as well. I'm actually more concerned with the way you handled that shit."

"But—" He put his hands up to stop me from arguing.

"Putting a sanction on a nigga is some boss shit, and I don't fault you at all for that. What I do have a problem with is yo' grown ass throwin' temper tantrums and shit. If you and yo' brother disagree on some shit and it comes to the point that you're goin' back and forth like some bitches, then you need to bring y'all asses here and we'll vote that shit out like a real democracy. Now can yo' hotheaded ass manage that?" he questioned, opening his hands before clasping them back together as he awaited my answer. I didn't want to have to involve our pops in any of our disagreements, but if that's what needed to be done, especially when it came to that nigga Julez, then I was willing to rock with it.

"I got you, Pops, man," I sighed, and his face split into a wide grin.

"That's what I like to hear." He gave Kash's stomach a squeeze that had his ass laughing, before setting him down on the floor. "Ayite, now take this lil' cock blockin' nigga with you. I'm tryna get some pussy tonight!"

CHAPTER ELEVEN
CA'MAHRI

"Come on, Ms. Bernice," I urged, reaching to help my last resident of the night out of her recliner. Usually, I would've had her in bed by now, but she'd insisted on watching *The Late Show* because Ari Lennox was on, and she swore that was her great-niece. I didn't believe that shit for a minute, and if it wasn't for the charting I needed to do, then her ass would've been in bed like everybody else.

"Don't rush me, girl! I'm tryna see my great-niece!" she huffed, swatting my hand away with her lips poked out since she didn't have her teeth in.

"You already saw her, Ms. Bernice, don't you remember?" It was really messed up how bad Alzheimer's affected her in the time that I'd been working there. Most nights she could barely remember her own name, and since she rarely got visits, she wouldn't have known one of her family members if they were right in her face. Confused, she looked up at me with squinted eyes, and my heart broke for her.

"I did?"

"Yes, she sung your favorite song too, girl!" I told her excitedly, and the lie had her giving me a toothless grin. After that, she allowed me to help her out of her chair and into the bathroom to help her prepare for bed. By the time I finally had her tucked in, her eyelids were drooping and I knew it wouldn't be long before she was snoring.

Since all of my work was finally done, I went to sit down behind the nurses' station and let out a content sigh once I did. After eight hours on my feet, it felt good to finally relax, and I was hoping that none of my call lights went off before the next shift arrived to take over. I planned to pull up a good book and read a little, but as soon as I went into the Kindle app, a text was coming through from Dinero. My lips instantly turned up into a smile seeing his name, and I hurried to open it up.

Dinero: What's good, beautiful? How your night going?

It was crazy how I'd only known him for such a short time, and he was already more concerned about me than a nigga I had spent six months with. Walt had never asked how my night was and sadly, I had gotten used to it. In the weeks we'd been talking, Dinero went out of his way to hit me up at least once a day to ask how I was doing, and he made sure to have me check in to let him know I was home on the nights I worked. It was out of character from what I knew of him, but it was also very sweet and kept a smile on my face.

Me: Nothing much, can't wait to get off tho', 'cause my feet are killing me, lol. How are you?

I watched the bubbles pop up indicating that he was texting back and raised a brow. I liked that he wasn't trying to play it super cool and take a long time replying the way that niggas liked to do. Since we'd been talking, I realized that Dinero wasn't like a lot of the other niggas I'd come across, and he wasn't nearly as mean as he'd been when we met. He was actually funny, and thoughtful, which I liked, but I also wasn't going to be a fool. I was well aware of how easy it was to get sucked in early and then a person's true colors appear and you're left looking a fool. Despite the butterflies Dinero was giving me, I fully planned to take my time and just enjoy myself for the time being.

Dinero: I'm cool...just got in the crib, but if you need me to I'll slide and rub those dogs for you, was his reply with the crying laughing emoji. I busted out laughing when I read that and the nurse shot me a look.

"Sorry, Gwen," I rushed to apologize and buried my head back into my phone, still giggling quietly as I typed a message back.

Me: You got me fucked up, my toes are pretty enough to put in your mouth, nigga, don't play with me!

Immediately, my phone started ringing with a FaceTime call from him and my eyes shot straight to Gwen, who was looking right at me already. I mumbled an apology and rushed to the bathroom down the hall, answering once I was far enough away.

"Pull them muhfuckas out right now, and they bet not have no corns, hang nails, chipped nail polish, or be throwing up gang signs either or I'm gon' roast the fuck out you!" he said, bringing his face close as hell to the camera as soon as the call connected, making a laugh bubble in my throat again.

"Oooooh, you really tryin' me right now! I ain't even off work yet, but I'll definitely let you see them if only to prove yo' mean ass wrong! What I get if they are pretty though?" I was cheesing hard as hell, taking in his handsome ass face. He smiled, making his already chinky eyes even more squinted, and ran a hand down his face. He'd told me a bit about the different businesses his family owned and how he bounced around overseeing them all when his brother couldn't, so I knew he was probably dog tired, or high.

"*If* yo' shit don't look like Myra's off *Martin*, then I'll give you a foot rub, but you gon' have to keep yo' socks on 'cause just because they're pretty don't mean they don't stink," he cracked, and my mouth fell open.

"Boy, my feet do not stink!"

"You ain't even proved that they don't look like deer hooves yet, one step at a time, now take yo' sock off." His ass was really trying to go in on my feet, and that only had me ready to bust his bubble.

"You know what?" I leaned against the sink and pulled off my shoe and then my sock, before smirking triumphantly as I flipped the camera around to my freshly pedicured toes. Since it was spring I decided to go with a cute pink French tip, and I had to admit that it looked good against my skin tone. "Soooo, what you got to say now, hater?" I wiggled my toes so he could get a better look.

"Shiiiiit, it looks like you got six toes on that muhfucka but other than that, I guess they look ayite."

"Okay, see now you bouta get it for real. Why don't you show me your toes? I bet yo' nails black and full of toe jam and ashy in between each toe!" I quipped, flipping the camera back around and putting my sock and shoe back on.

"Nahh, not mine! I go let them Chinese muhfuckas work on my shit, and I make sure I use lotion. You must be talkin' 'bout yo' other nigga," he quickly denied, but didn't make a move to show me. My cheeks instantly hiked up at him basically saying we were together, even though I knew he was joking.

"I don't have another nigga, Dinero."

"Good answer, 'cause I don't wanna have to fuck you up." He tried to look serious but a smirk played at the corners of his mouth, giving him away.

"Whatever you say, Dinero. Now back to my foot rub you promised me. When I'm gettin' that?"

"Maaaan, I got you. What time you get off?" His voice

dipped and butterflies filled my stomach. I hadn't seen him in person since the night at the club a couple weeks ago, so I was instantly both excited and nervous at the prospect of being alone with him.

"I can leave in thirty," I rushed to say, making his fine ass chuckle, and inwardly chastised myself for sounding so thirsty.

"Ayite, I'll meet you there."

"Okay, see you in a bit," I simpered as I hung up. As soon as his face was no longer on the screen, I began to panic though. Was I moving too fast allowing him to come over? Dinero had been a perfect gentleman so far, but I knew he had the capabilities to ease himself right between my legs. What if he thought that's what I was inviting him over for? Everybody knew niggas couldn't give massages without letting their hands slip and if I was being honest, I didn't know if my will was strong enough to stop him. "You're trippin' for nothin', bitch," I mumbled, putting my phone in the pockets of my scrubs and then rubbing some hand sanitizer on before I returned to the nurses' station.

Of course, the last ten minutes felt like an hour as I finished the walk through with the CNA coming on. After giving her report, I grabbed my bag and headed to the other unit so I could speak to my mama before I left. I found her behind the nurses' station preparing her cart for the night and as soon as she saw me, her face split into a grin.

"Hey, baby!" she gushed, pulling me in for a hug. "You look like you bouta run up outta here!"

"Hey, Ma, you already know, 'cause they'll mess around and ask you to stay over real quick."

"And will!" she agreed, and I had to laugh at her using me and Camille's lingo. Our mama didn't look a day over thirty, and despite her actual age of forty-five, she stayed up on the latest slang, fashion, and music. Her looks and personality often had people thinking we were all sisters whenever we went out together, and that only pumped her head up even more. She loved to hear that she didn't look old enough to have two grown children, and our daddy wasn't any better. They both seemed to have aged backward and swore they were as young as me and Camille. "Anyway, it's supposed to be warm Thursday. You and Walt should come by. I been trying to call your sister so she won't be whining about not getting invited, but that lil' heffa ain't been answering her phone."

The mention of Walt had my eye twitching. I hadn't gotten a chance to tell my mama about us breaking up, and it was mostly because my parents hated him just as much as Camille. While my daddy was more vocal about his dislike, my mama tried to be supportive of our relationship, which was probably why she'd extended the invite to him. Blowing out a deep breath, I leaned closer so the nosy ass people standing around wouldn't hear. "Me and Walt broke up, Ma."

"Thank God!" she shouted, raising her hands in the air in exaggeration.

"Ma!"

"What! I'm happy, shoot! You know I try to let you and Camille live y'all's lives, but I was starting to get nervous, honey!" With a raised brow, she finally lowered her voice like she wanted to be secretive now. "So, what happened? That nigga ain't cheat, did he? 'Cause I'll have Darnell go over there and beat his ass! I know yo' daddy would take the day off for that ass whoopin'!"

"Oh my gosh, no, he didn't cheat. It was something else, but I don't really have time to tell you everything right now. I'm supposed to be meeting a friend in a lil' bit." Her eyes bucked and she gave me a knowing grin.

"Oooh, I know what that means. I see you, girl, I see you! That's the easiest way to get over a man, I'm tellin' you!"

"Okay, girl," my voice shrilled awkwardly. "I'm gone see you later."

"Alright, bye baby." She waved me off and got back to work. *Thank God!*

After she held me up, I was finally able to leave the building and I sent a quick text to Dinero to make sure he hadn't left his house yet. He let me know that he was just getting in his car too, so I knew I didn't have much time. Without letting my car warm up, I sped home, dropped my things, and hurried to take a shower. I'd just finished putting on a tan two-piece lounge set from Shein when he knocked, and I breathed a sigh of relief. My freshly done knotless braids were loose and sweeping my back as I switched to the door to let him in, lighting a few candles along the way. I knew without a doubt that I was looking good and smelling even better after having sprayed on some of my Carolina Herrera Very Good Girl perfume.

"Damn. Hey, beautiful." Dinero eyed me from head to toe in appreciation, and I had to admit that I was thinking the same thing. He looked like he'd just climbed out of his barber's chair right before he pulled up and not only that, but he was dressed in a gray sweatsuit that had his dick print on full display. I didn't know what cologne he had on, but it was heavenly and when he pulled me in for a hug, I damn near melted. Towering over my five-foot-five frame, he wrapped his strong arms around me and dropped a soft kiss on my neck, making me shudder. *Lord, give me strength!*

CHAPTER TWELVE
DINERO

Ca'Mahri's soft ass body felt so good pressed against mine that I almost didn't want to let her go. She'd answered the door looking thick as hell and smelling sweet enough to eat, like she was trying to see how long I could last without putting this dick in her life. Normally, that's exactly what I would've been on, but the more I got to know her ass the more she had me going back on my word. I didn't miss the little moan she'd let out when my lips touched her skin, but I wasn't going to call her out. Instead, I released her with a wide grin, pleased to know that she was feeling the heat as much as I was.

"Yo' ass look tired as hell," I commented, looking her over once again and causing her to give me one of those little girlie shoves that didn't move me an inch.

"Because I am, so come on before I mess around and fall asleep on you." Slipping her hand in mine, she pulled me further inside and twisted around to lock the door before guiding me through her crib. I nodded in approval at how put together it was as I enjoyed the strong scent of sugar cookies that permeated throughout. Everything in there was super girly, decorated in pink or white with splashes of gold here and there. She even had pink LED lights glowing from behind her flat screen with candles in various areas, so the living room had an intimate vibe.

Stopping at her pink ass couch, she plopped down and I took a seat next to her since the other end was covered in a bunch of decorative pillows. She wasted no time lying back and throwing her feet into my lap with a lazy grin on her face.

"I'm ready when you are," she sang, wiggling her toes, and I feigned a look of disgust as I lifted her foot with two fingers. Truthfully, her shit was even prettier in person and looked like she'd just gotten them done. I loved shit like that and how well Ca'Mahri took care of herself. She was always well put together and that shit was a major turn on. "Stop playin', Dinero!"

"Ayite, I quit." I laughed at the pout on her face and finally started rubbing her small ass foot. Her face instantly relaxed and she closed her eyes with a soft moan, letting me know that what I was doing felt good. "Maaan, you really bouta fall asleep on me?" My tone was full of teasing, as I put more pressure on the ball of her foot.

"Hmmm, no, I'm up," she lied, struggling to lift her lids. "We can watch the new *Texas Chainsaw*." I peeped her trying to stifle a yawn as she searched for the remote, but didn't call her out. As much as we talked, I was well aware of her work schedule and how draining her job could be. If didn't nobody understand that shit, I did, having to run multiple businesses both legal and illegal. My fucked-up hours had been the main reason why we still hadn't gone on an official date yet. The first night I had to cancel right before I was set to pick her up because some niggas had tried to rob our most lucrative trap, and the second time one of our duplexes had a flood in the basement. Ca'Mahri was understanding both times, though, so I knew I'd have to make it up with something special and real soon too.

"Yeah, I can fuck with that," I agreed, switching to her other foot while she pulled the movie up.

"You want a drink or something? I got some Minute Maid and bottled water. I don't really drink pop like that." I could already tell just from her glowing skin and clear complexion that she wasn't a fan of the sugary drink, but hearing her say it was sexy as hell. Or it could've just been me being on some thirsty shit when it came to her.

"Nah, I'm good, baby." She had already been preparing to stand but as soon as I declined, she rested back against the couch with a slick smirk.

"Oh, I done got bumped up to baby now?" she questioned, calling me out. Honestly, the term had just flown from my mouth naturally and I hadn't thought much about it, but seeing that it was another way to put a smile on her face was all the more reason to say it again.

"Shiiit, you got yo' crusty ass feet in my lap, you gone be considered baby, honey, bae, all that shit." I chuckled, but I was only half joking.

"You gon' stop talkin' 'bout my feet." Huffing, she tried to slide them off me but I held on firmly to the one in my hands.

"Man, I'm just fuckin' with you, sit yo' ass back," I ordered sternly, unfazed by her fake ass attitude. We had a staring contest for a few seconds before she finally relaxed back against the couch with a suck of her teeth. Now her eyes were wide open and fixed on the screen, and I had to laugh at how stubborn she was being. I knew damn well she couldn't really be mad about a couple of jokes, but her body language said it all. She was definitely in her fake feelings. "So you mad?" I quizzed, giving her foot a little squeeze.

"Nope." She made sure to put emphasis on the p, making the word end with a pop, and I smirked before pulling her legs until she was damn near on top of me. "Gone, Dinero!" Her little mean ass fought hard not to giggle but lost as I started tickling her.

"You still mad?" I paused briefly to ask.

"I told you I wasn't mad!" she gasped, trying to catch her breath, but I wasn't trying to hear that shit. "Okay, okay! I'm not mad anymore!"

"You sure?"

"Yes, I'm sure!" I had to admit that I didn't want to let up on her, mainly because I liked her being so close to a nigga. It seemed like her small frame fit perfectly in my lap and I wasn't in a rush for her to move. I looked down into her pretty ass face, surmising that she looked the most beautiful to me when her face was void of makeup, and before I could stop myself, I was covering her lips with mine. Whimpering, she kissed me back and melted into my chest as her tongue invaded my mouth. My dick started waking up as I grabbed a handful of her ass, and she caressed the back of my head, getting more into it. Shit was heating up quickly and the movie was completely forgotten about, but the chiming of my burner had me pulling away with a groan. That phone was always on and whenever it rang there was some business that needed my attention. Ca'Mahri sat up wide eyed, and I felt her body tense when I answered.

"Nigga, this better be life threatening!" I snapped.

"Aye, boss, it's some niggas over here insisting they see you," one of my young workers named Snoop informed me, instantly making my face tight. Who would be trying to talk to me on the block at this time of night? I immediately knew it couldn't have been anybody I fucked with because they'd know better, and that had me even more heated.

"The fuck! You know I don't do business there, and how them niggas even know where my shit at anyway?" I gently lifted Ca'Mahri off me and stood, waiting to hear what his ass had to say because if it wasn't adequate, somebody was getting fucked up.

"They with Walt, but I already told them you wasn't open for discussions like this. They're steady saying they not leaving 'til you get here." Hearing Walt's name had me ready to spit fire. I'd already warned his ass, and now he was bringing randoms to my spots like he didn't know he could die.

Sighing, I looked regretfully at Ca'Mahri, who was still watching my every move with clear displeasure written on her face. "Ayite, man, I'll be there in twenty." She rolled her eyes as I hung up and finally stood, trying to walk past me, but I grabbed her up in a hug.

"Come on so you can get to where you're goin'," she said dryly, and if I didn't know I had fucked up before, I knew that shit now.

"Don't be mad, baby, if this shit didn't demand my attention—"

"You wouldn't go, I already know," she finished the same sentence I'd given both times I was called away on business, making me feel bad as hell, but not bad enough to stay. I wasn't used to being torn between business and pleasure, so my first instinct was always to play my position and handle business before anything else. I didn't want to keep disappointing her but if things between us went any further, then it was something she'd have to get used to.

"I'ma make this shit up to you, ayite?" I promised, but she only grunted in response and turned away so that the kiss I tried to give landed on her cheek. Unfortunately, I didn't have time to try and smooth shit out, but I made a mental note to send her some roses as I left her standing there.

* * *

I'd called Cash on the way over and he must have sped over
because he pulled up right after I did with his gun already in
hand. Just like Snoop had said, it was about ten niggas just
standing out front, but as soon as we walked up they turned
around to face us. The nigga I'm assuming was in charge stood
front and center with a still beat-up Walt at his side, and I
fought off the urge to laugh at how bad Ca'Mahri had fucked
his ass up. His jaw tightened the closer I got, but I ignored him
and focused my attention on the man of the hour.

Right away I could tell that there was some relation
between the two, and that solidified even further that I was
about to deny him whatever he was asking for. "Dinero and
Cash muhfuckin' Banks! I'm honored y'all decided to come
meet with a nigga, truly." He grinned widely, palming his chest
with one hand and reaching out for a dap with the other. Lip
curled in disgust, I intentionally crossed my hands in front of
me, unmoved by his weak ass greeting. Clearly the nigga was a
dick rider just like Walt, and if it wouldn't have caused a bunch
of unnecessary attention, I would've had my workers blow
them down right there.

"Did you have a reason for pulling all this extra shit to get
us here or you just tryna be on some groupie shit?" I questioned, glaring at him. Shock registered on his face but he
quickly recovered and his grin returned.

"Damn, that was disrespectful as fuck, but I get it," his
crazy ass said, taking the exact same stance as me, hand over
fist in front of him and legs planted firmly. "Look, my name's
Lox and I run outta Wisconsin, but unfortunately, my supply
has dried up so I'm in need of a new plug. I been tryna send
this goofy ass nigga to holla at y'all for a minute on my behalf,
but obviously you can't send a boy to do a man's job." He shot a

contemptuous look at Walt, whose eyes turned downward from the heat. I heard Cash scoff beside me and knew we were thinking the same thing.

"We straight." He shrugged casually, making the nigga Lox's face crumble. No doubt he wasn't expecting us to tell his ass no, but he should've known better. Not only did we never fuck with randoms, but the way he introduced himself in addition to being related to Walt had left a bad taste in my mouth. The men standing behind him all looked at each other uneasily as this nigga released a bitter chuckle.

"That's it? Y'all not even gone hear me out?" he questioned in disbelief.

"Nigga—!" Cash went to step in his face, but I held him back as multiple guns were drawn from the porch and Lox's men all pulled their weapons in response.

"Aye, y'all niggas put that shit away!" I barked, and they begrudgingly did what I said. Lox's men followed suit once my glare landed on them. Unsure of what to do, they looked to Lox, who didn't seem happy at all by their confusion, but he still gave them a stiff nod. I waited until they'd put their guns up before turning to my brother. "You good?"

He kept his eyes on Lox, jaw clenching in unspoken rage. If it was up to him we'd be putting a bullet in that nigga's head on the spot, but we couldn't do no shit like that. Calling his name seemed to snap him out of the trance he was in, and an evil smirk crossed his face. "I'm chillin'."

"Ayite, Lox, you heard the man." That nigga looked pissed and on the verge of trying to put up a fight, but thankfully, he took the smart route and walked away. Silently, I kept my eyes on them until their tail lights disappeared around the corner, already knowing this wasn't the last I'd be seeing of that nigga. I just hoped he wasn't dumb enough to make an enemy out of us.

CHAPTER THIRTEEN
CAMILLE

"Ugh!" Ca'Mahri grunted, rolling her eyes at her phone. She'd been in a funky ass mood for the last couple of weeks because of Dinero, even though she tried to pretend she wasn't pressed.

"You know you could just answer." I shrugged, making her shoot an evil look my way.

"Not miss checklist telling me to talk to a nigga that's clearly playing games? If you were talking to somebody and they kept getting called away on 'business' you'd cut them off too. Don't even front," she called me out, and I couldn't even argue facts. I was well aware of the hours that a successful man kept, but I was also a firm believer in making time for what and who you wanted. My cut-off game was strong when it came to these niggas, but at the same time I wasn't as tender hearted as my sister. The fact that she hadn't immediately just blocked him instead of denying his calls and messages told me that she wanted to see him trying to get in touch with her. Shit probably had the bitch's heart fluttering like this was a romantic comedy.

"True, you already know I don't play, but yo' soft ass. You ain't even blocked the nigga yet so you must still wanna hear from him," I quipped, pursing my lips with a raised brow.

"Don't nobody wanna talk to that nigga!" her lying ass huffed with a flick of her wrist.

"Whatever you say, girl." I chuckled.

I really didn't have any room to be talking with the way Cash had me open, but at the same time, his ass was crazy. If I even tried to ignore that nigga there was no telling what he'd do, his ass had already kidnapped me. As if he knew I was thinking about him, my phone rang and his name flashed across the screen.

"Hey," I cooed, unable to stop myself from smiling. That shit instantly caught Ca'Mahri's attention and she gave me a knowing look. Turning my back to her, I walked off a little bit so she wouldn't hear my conversation, even though I still felt her burning a hole in the side of my head.

"What's up, what yo' fine ass doin'?" he asked, sounding like he was in the middle of a party. Loud ass music was blasting in the background along with a bunch of shrieks, and I instantly caught an attitude. Granted, we hadn't put a label on what it was we called ourselves doing, but I wasn't in the business of sharing either.

"I'm at the mall with Ca'Mahri. What you doing? Why it sound like you at a damn party?" My nose turned up as I asked, and his rude ass fell into a fit of laughter.

"Yooo! I know Camille the playa ain't sounding jealous! Damn, I ain't know I had it like that." Humor was evident in his voice, making me even more irritated that he hadn't answered my question and that he found the shit funny in the first place. I couldn't even front, I'd quickly gotten spoiled by the attention and good dick that Cash was showering me with, and I damn sure didn't like the thought of him giving any of it to another bitch.

"Haha, but you still ain't dropped your location tho'." He laughed again like I'd told a damn joke, but the sound of a woman's voice seeming way too close if I could hear had me ready to spit nails.

"Would you like *anything* else?"

"Aww, hell naw! Tell that bitch you don't need shit from her! Who is that, a server talkin' like that?" I snapped, walking further away from Ca'Mahri's nosy ass. Really, it was a damn shame to be acting this way after only a month, but I couldn't even stop myself from burning up with jealousy.

"Brooo, you trippin'! I'll send you the address, but don't bring yo' ass up here actin' a fool and shit."

"Mmmhmm, hurry up and send it." Scoffing, I hung up in his face and tapped my foot as I waited for his location to pop up. I was half expecting him to not even send it, but a second later my phone dinged and I instantly frowned, wondering what his ass was doing all the way out in fucking Winnetka. It had sounded like he was at a damn strip club, but there damn sure wasn't any that I knew of out in the plush suburb that his location said. Then again, Cash and Dinero were young rich niggas, and probably had friends who threw parties at mansions all the time. Shit, for all I knew, it was his damn party! I was definitely about to find out though!

Dropping the items I was holding on a nearby display table, I switched over to where Ca'Mahri was still browsing. "Come on, I need you to run me somewhere quick." I didn't even wait for her to agree before snatching her arm and pulling her away from the store. The entire way through the mall and out to the parking lot she was trying to ask me questions, but I was laser focused and on a mission. I'd tried to keep things between me and Cash on a sexual level and not allow my feelings to get involved, but he'd insisted on pursuing me. Now he was going to have to deal with the monster he'd unleashed!

"Girl, where you got me drivin' to?" Ca'Mahri fussed after I'd given her directions to the get on the expressway.

"To go beat Cash's ass," I said, shrugging casually, and her eyes damn near popped out of her head as she did a double take. "Bitch, watch the road!" I was hoping that would stop her from giving me the knowing look she currently had on her face.

"Ooooh, you really like him!"

"I mean, I wouldn't say all that." My lying ass averted my eyes but still felt her staring at me with a psychotic grin. "I'm just not bouta let him play with me."

"Awwww! You're blushing!" she gushed, poking my cheek with her finger, and I resisted the urge to bite that motherfucker off. I didn't like the fact that I was in my feelings over Cash. Especially considering that he had at least three strikes against him on my list of no-no's. Besides being way too good in bed, his ass had a young child, which meant that he had a baby mama that wasn't too far behind. The only thing working in his favor was the fact that his son basically lived with him, and as far as I knew, his mama had been MIA. We'd been together a lot over the last month, and I hadn't witnessed her blowing up his phone or doing any of the other crazy shit I knew baby mamas to do. That gave me a little bit of reassurance, but now he was acting up and about to see why niggas didn't play with me.

"Gon' bitch!" I smacked her hand away and her silly ass only giggled. She was clearly getting way too much joy out of this shit, and that only irritated me more. Thankfully, with the way she drove we made the half-hour trip in almost twenty minutes and instantly, we both were in awe of the fancy houses that lined the streets.

"Daaaaamn, who live out here?" she wanted to know, shooting me a confused look as we stopped in front of the address that Cash had sent me. A huge black, wrought-iron gate stopped us from getting inside, and I realized I'd have to call him to open it. Just as I prepared to press his contact, an intercom box crackled to life.

"Guests of Mr. Banks, Camille and Ca'Mahri?" a Hispanic woman came on the line and asked, making us share a look, before Ca'Mahri leaned out of her window.

"Uhh, yeah."

"Welcome, please come to the first house and someone will let you inside," she said, and the gate slowly creaked open, granting us entrance. We drove a short distance up the winding road and came upon a mansion that could've easily fit both of our apartments inside with room to spare. As Ca'Mahri pulled up the circular drive, I made out two other mansions further in the distance that were just as opulent. These people clearly had money, money, and I suddenly felt a little uneasy as we came to a stop behind at least fifteen other cars, all of which were luxury.

"Uhh, bitch, you sure about this?" Ca'Mahri's scary ass looked between me and the house with wide eyes.

"Not really, but we're already here so let's go," I sighed, reaching for the handle and stepping out before I could change my mind. We'd made it this far and although I would probably tone down the heat I had for that nigga, he was still going to get it if I saw any funny shit inside. I could already hear the loud ass music coming from the back and that just further egged me on. My heels clicked against the pavement as I walked to the door with Ca'Mahri lagging behind. *Scary ass!* I thought, lifting my hand to ring the bell, but the double doors came open and a woman that was around my age stood on the other side in a maid uniform. She silently sized me up, before forcing a smile and extending her arm for us to enter. Rolling my eyes, I strolled past her rude ass and waited for my sister to catch up. As soon as she came in and saw the maid, her silly self did a damn curtsy and despite my mood, I busted out laughing.

"Yo' ass crazy, girl! Why I'm the fuck did you just curtsy at that lady?" I cackled, linking my arm through hers and following the sound of music to the back of the house.

"Well, what else was I s'posed to do, hell? I ain't never met a maid before." I just shook my head as we reached the kitchen where the patio doors were open and a buffet of food was laid out on a long ass table. The scent of good BBQ and seafood filled the air, instantly making my stomach rumble. Ca'Mahri wasted no time using some of the hand sanitizer on the table before filling a bowl up with some of the fruit salad.

"What, I'm hungry!" she huffed, stuffing a round piece of cantaloupe in her mouth. Rolling my eyes at her greedy ass, I continued to look for Cash among the people that were moving around between the kitchen and backyard.

"Señor Kash, watch out!" I heard somebody yell just as a small body crashed into me, and I looked down into the most adorable little face. It didn't take a rocket scientist to know that I was staring into the face of Cash's mini, and that fact was proven when he hit me with the same grin his father always wore. "I'm so sorry, señora!" A maid rushed over trying to help him up, but he clung to my leg mischievously.

"It's ok. I got him," I told her, reaching down to pick him up and was surprised that he allowed it. Just from the uneasiness on the woman's face as I lifted him into my arms, I knew everyone was overprotective of him, and that was probably because he was bad as hell. She eyed me for a second like she was waiting for him to act up, before finally walking away with a sigh. Ignoring her, I put my attention back on the little boy, marveling over how adorable he was with hair was braided into four long plaits that looked so soft, I had to stop myself from touching them. He was rocking a royal blue sweatshirt and light-wash jeans with matching Jordan's, looking just like one of those Instagram model babies. "Hey, cutie, what's your name?"

"I'm Kash! What's you name?" he chirped, tilting his head up at me, and my heart melted in my chest. I wasn't ever supposed to be hit this hard with baby fever, but I couldn't help wanting to just squeeze him.

"I'm Camille," I told him, watching as his face twisted up in confusion before he repeated it, completely missing the first letter, but the way his little voice grew high pitched at the end was hilarious.

"Amillll!"

"Yeah, you got it!" I gushed, flashing all thirty-two of my damn teeth as I tickled his little belly. Seeing that his son was there kind of calmed me down, and I no longer felt the need to show my ass, even though I still hadn't laid eyes on Cash.

Ca'Mahri cleared her throat beside me trying to be funny, and I twisted away from her, heading toward the open doors leading into the backyard. It was a lot more people back there, either huddled up in conversation or dancing to the Jagged Edge that was playing. Kash immediately started wiggling to get down as soon as I stepped out onto the concrete path, so I put him on the ground and he was off again. I kept my eyes on him until he reached one of the older couples that were out there dancing, before surveying the area for Cash.

"How yo' fine ass slip past me?" I shuddered, hearing that nigga's voice and having his body pressed against mine as his cologne tickled my nose. Turning around, I didn't put up a fight when he wrapped his arm around my waist. He looked high as hell with low red eyes and a big goofy grin on his face.

"Probably 'cause you was in there doin' somethin' you ain't have no business doin'!" I said smartly, even though I knew at this point that he'd set me up. It didn't look like there was anybody in attendance that wasn't family or a close friend, besides the maids moving about, so maybe I had overreacted. His grin widened at the accusation, and he buried his face in my neck, leaving a wet kiss there.

"You don't even believe that for real," he scoffed, seeing right through my bullshit. "Yo' jealous ass hungry? We got all types of shit in there."

"First of all, I wasn't jealous. I was just gone smack you and whatever bitch was in yo' face! Matter fact, where she at anyway? I bet it was the one who let us in!" I sucked my teeth, straining to see if her hating ass was anywhere in sight.

"You ready to fight a damn maid? Yo' ass wild." He threw his head back laughing, and I had to join him because it did sound a little crazy.

"Well, you shouldn't have sounded like you was at a damn strip club instead of a family gathering."

"That's my freaky ass parents listening to them damn baby-making songs. It's their anniversary so they been trippin' all day." His forehead bunched and he shuddered like just the thought was gross. Finding out that this get together was actually an anniversary party for his parents had me sighing in relief that I hadn't came in slinging bitches like I planned to. "Here they aggravating asses go right here," he grumbled, and I instantly tensed up. The last thing I was prepared to do that day was meet his son and his parents and suddenly, I was self-conscious, but it was already too late. Cash's focus landed just over my head and I heard a woman chuckle behind me.

"Who's your friend, Cash?"

CHAPTER FOURTEEN

CASH

Camille's reaction to my folks was funny as hell considering that she always put up a tough front. She was damn near shaking in her boots as I spun her around so that she was face to face with my mama, who was holding Kash's little bad ass.

"Hi, I'm—"

"That's Amille!" Kash surprised us all by shouting and pointing a tiny finger her way. Smiling, she extended her hand to my mama while I tried to figure out when they ran across each other. As big as my parents' house was, there wasn't no telling, but I was digging the fact that he seemed to like her already.

"Yes, I'm Camille."

"It's nice to meet you," my mama's friendly ass gushed, shaking her hand vigorously. "I'm Keshia and this is my husband, Kendrick. I guess you've already met this lil' guy." She poked his belly, sending him into a fit of laughter.

"Maaan, you need to put his big ass down!" I mumbled, taking a drink of my beer.

"Shut up!"

"Shut yo' ass up!" my mama and Camille snapped at the same time. "Ooh, I like her! Come on, baby, have you ate yet?" She looped her arm through Camille's and led her off while my pops just shook his head and laughed.

"You know you done fucked up, right?" his old ass said, walking in the same direction they'd gone in.

"Aye man, Dinero's girl is here too while y'all tryna tag team mine!" I shouted after them, but their asses continued on until they'd disappeared through the patio doors. Even as I talked shit, though, I was cheesing hard as hell. My family's opinion meant a lot to me, and the fact that Camille had already won over my granny, my folks, and Kash was a good ass sign. I already knew they were going to be gone for a hot little minute, so I returned to my seat by the pool and kicked my feet up. The weather was being kind as fuck and delivering a light breeze that felt amazing enough to put my high ass to sleep. Unfortunately, that shit wasn't ever gone happen with my people walking around and getting on my damn nerves. If I heard *how you doin', baby?* one more time, I knew I was going to snap. After I got rid of one of the great-aunts on my mama's side, I walked in the house and warmed my granny up a plate. My pops had sent her upstairs to rest a while ago, but I was sure she was still up and needing some food. By now it had been almost a half hour since my folks had ran off with Camille and I still had yet to see her, but I did peep Dinero shuffling Ca'Mahri into one of the guest rooms. *Ole slick ass nigga!*

Knocking, I cracked the door to the room my granny was in and used one hand to cover my eyes as I stood in the doorway. "You decent in here, Dorothea?" I teased, waiting for her to give me the okay to come inside.

"Why in the hell wouldn't I be decent, boy!" She wasted no time going off on me. She'd been testy as hell lately and it didn't help that my pops was trying to treat her like a baby, in her words.

"See, I was just bringin' you some food, old lady!" I laughed, stepping fully into the room and holding the plate out to her. My pops had her pillows all around her and had even put some under her feet.

"I got yo' old!" She struggled to get to me with her face balled up.

"Ayite, ayite! My bad, just sit back before you fall or something and Kendrick try to beat my ass!" She glared at me but stopped trying to get up, and I set the plate next to her on the nightstand with a diet Pepsi next to it. That shit instantly had her lighting up like a Christmas tree just like I knew it would. My granny loved her some diet Pepsi, even though the doctor had told her to limit how much she drank. Slipping out of my shoes, I dropped down into the sitting chair in the corner and crossed my legs over the matching ottoman.

"Awww, thanks baby!" she gushed, all sugary sweet like she hadn't just went off on me, and the next thing I heard was her cracking her pop open.

"You're welcome, Grams. I got another surprise for you too." She raised her brow questioningly but was already shoveling a forkful of greens in her mouth. "Yo' friend Camille downstairs, but yo' son and his wife ran off with her and Kash, so I don't know if she'll get a chance to come up here and see you."

"I'll go find her! Kendrick's ass can't keep me locked up here all night!" she fussed, and I knew I'd started some shit at that point. Finding out about Camille's presence was for sure going to have her making her way back to the party regardless of what my pops was saying.

"Ayite, he gone get his damn belt!"

"I wished the fuck he would! I'm his mama! You probably

ain't never seen yo' daddy get his ass whooped before, but if he start with that bullshit I'm gone fuck his thick ass up!" She frowned, making me laugh hard as hell. I could picture her trying to fight that nigga and almost wanted to see her really beat his ass. It didn't take her long to start talking about something else while she ate, and I half listened and scrolled social media.

Halfway down my Instagram feed, I got pissed off seeing my baby mama had posted a picture of the O'Hare expressway sign, and that shit had been up for two days! I just knew she hadn't brought her ass home from vacation and didn't come see our son! I told my grandma I'd be right back and hurried out of the room, pressing send on her contact along the way. It seemed like it took forever for her baldheaded ass to answer but when she did, she had the nerve to sound pissed off at me.

"What, Cash!"

"I know yo' stupid ass better take that fuckin' aggression out yo' voice talkin' to me!" I barked, wishing I could reach through the phone and wring her ratchet ass neck. "Why the fuck you been home two days and ain't even called to check on Kash?" The fact that I even had to ask her some shit like that had me heated, because I'd been understanding as fuck when she said she needed a getaway, but now she was testing me. Shorty was a whole deadbeat out here and I couldn't wait until I caught up with her, because I was damn sure going to pay a couple hood bitches to beat her ass.

"First of all, nigga, I was only out that way for a few hours. I didn't even have enough time to stop through there because I was ridin' with some other people." I couldn't believe that I had procreated with the bitch on the other end of the phone. Vernique had always been a little ratchet, but she'd never gone this far before.

"Bitch—!" I bit my lip to stop myself from saying too much

when Camille appeared at the top of the stairs, calling me with Kash right on her heels. She had been smiling, but the closer she got, her brows bunched seeing the aggravation I was sure was evident on my face. I appreciated that she immediately steered Kash in the opposite direction, even though it was too late because my stupid ass baby mama had already heard her.

"I know that ain't no bitch around Kash! You really got yo' nerve tryna talk shit to me when you lettin' random ass bitches around him!"

"She ain't no fuckin' random!"

"I ain't met her! Shit, I ain't even know yo' stupid ass was fuckin' with somebody!" she shouted, and I had to look at the phone after hearing her say some dumb shit like that. Instead of replying, I just pressed the end button before I fucked around and punched a hole in the wall.

It took me a few minutes to get myself under control before I returned to the room with my grandma. She watched me cross the room to where my shoes were and sit down to put them back on, and I could tell she wanted to say something. "Gon' say what you gotta say, Granny," I sighed without looking up.

"Tuh! You already know what I'm gone say! Same thing I told yo' daddy, and that's watch who you droppin' babies off in!" I damn near choked on my spit as my head snapped in her direction, and her old ass just bucked her eyes at me.

"Brooo, Dorothea, yo' ass trippin'!"

"I ain't trippin', you trippin'! Skeetin' in that ditzy ass girl! If Camille ain't yo' next baby mama, I'm disowning yo' black ass! Now send her up here, so I can say hey." She leaned back against her pillows with her hands folded like she hadn't just said some wild ass shit, and I chuckled.

"Ayite, I got you, Granny." Shaking my head, I grabbed her

trash and left to find Camille for her like she'd told me to. I wasn't going to let Vernique fuck up the rest of my day. I'd just deal with her when the opportunity presented itself, and I was hoping that wouldn't be any time soon.

CHAPTER FIFTEEN
CA'MAHRI

I had been running from Dinero's ass since Camille left me in the kitchen to bond with her stepchild and he'd finally caught up to me. His fine ass cornered me at the top of their winding staircase and shoved me into one of the many guestrooms. Holding a firm grip on my arm, he locked the door before releasing me and looming over me with a look that could kill. We stood staring at each other in angry silence, and I was just waiting on what he had to say. He surprised me, though, and covered my mouth with his.

Before I knew it, he had me laid out on the huge four-poster, king-sized bed with my legs wrapped around his neck. After giving me back-to-back orgasms that had me unable to walk for a good thirty minutes, he warned me to not go without answering his phone calls again.

That had been two days ago, and I was still having after-shocks just thinking about the way he'd used his tongue on me. The problem was now that I hadn't heard from him since, and it was to the point that I was ready to call his ass! *Grimy ass nigga!* I knew he'd done the shit on purpose so that now I was waiting on him to get in touch with me and not the other way around.

"Girl, what's wrong with you? You been over there huffin' and puffin' the whole shift," my coworker Roquelle asked, looking at me in fake concern. I was sure she was just trying to be nosy since I didn't go around like everyone else and tell all my damn business.

"Nothin', just looking at the new schedule," I lied, and even though the look on her face said she didn't believe me, she still started going on and on about her schedule. With the focus off me, I went back to scrolling Facebook. I was in the middle of commenting under Camille's drunk in love ass post when an email came through from the hiring manager at Rush Hospital. It had been a minute since I'd put in my application and had an interview, and I had honestly figured I didn't get the position and forgot all about it with so much shit going on in my life. Seeing their name in my email, though, had me rushing to open it with my heart pounding in my chest. There were so many pros to working at Rush. I'd be with my sister and Noelle, they paid more, and the best part was that they did tuition reimbursement so I'd have help paying to get my RN. I had been wanting to advance in the nursing field for years, it just never seemed like the right time, but I was finally committed to getting it done. Saying a silent prayer, I opened the email and had to stop myself from jumping out of my seat doing a little dance. They were offering me the position with damn near double the pay because of my experience.

I immediately snatched a piece of paper from one of the notebooks on the desk so I could write out a week's notice to my current job. If it wasn't for the fact that my mama still worked there I wouldn't have even given them that, but I couldn't leave her there to deal with the fallout of me doing no calls, no shows until they realized I quit. Plus, as much as I hated most of the staff, I couldn't do my fellow CNA's like that. I kept my letter short and to the point, making sure to put my last actual working date on there. By the time the next shift arrived and got their report, I was rushing to catch my mama so I could tell her the good news.

"Girrrrrl, guess what!" I huddled up next to where she stood at her cart preparing for the night, and she smiled widely seeing my excitement.

"Well, hey to you too."

"Hey, Ma....now guess what?" I asked again, almost bouncing from how excited I was, and she rolled her eyes with a chuckle.

"What, girl?"

"I got the job at Ruuuuush!" I shrieked, and her eyes widened as she grabbed me up into a hug.

"Awww, congratulations! I'm so happy for you, when do you start? Will you be working with your sister and Noelle?" she shot out back-to-back questions, making sure to keep her voice low since we'd gained the attention of everyone at the nurses' station. I spent the next fifteen minutes filling her in on everything I knew so far about the position, before she had to start her shift, but I promised to stop by sometime in the next week to visit her and my daddy.

On the way out of the building, I stopped to drop off my resignation in HR's drop box before calling Camille to let her know I'd be starting with them soon, but the bitch didn't answer. I figured she was up under Cash's ass as always and just left her a message to call me back.

Pulling up outside my house, I snatched up my work bag and prepared to get out just as my phone vibrated in my hand with a FaceTime call from Dinero. I started not to even answer after the way he'd done me the last time we saw each other, but I wasn't trying to find out what he'd do to me if I didn't pick up like he told me to.

"Hello." I made sure my attitude was evident as I answered, rolling my eyes with a long sigh, but he didn't seem fazed at all.

"I'm glad yo' ass know how to follow directions." He smirked into the camera, looking high as hell, and I realized he was out in a car judging from the way the streetlights kept flashing across his face.

"Not so much directions, more like an order." I shrugged smartly, causing his grin to widen. "Anyway, I just got in from work so if you don't mind, I'ma call you tomorrow."

"Nah, that ain't gone work."

"Excuse me?"

"I said you callin' me tomorrow ain't gone work," he repeated slowly, like I had a comprehension problem instead of just not liking what he'd said. Despite there not being anything funny about the situation, I couldn't help laughing at the nigga's audacity. He wanted me to rearrange my schedule when he'd canceled on me twice and left my company for some shit he still hadn't explained yet.

"That's unfortunate, *Dinero*, but I'm trying to get an early start, so like I said, I'll call you tomorrow."

"Maaaan, turn around," he ordered, hanging up in my face, with his rude ass. I glanced in the rearview but didn't see anything besides the same empty ass street I'd seen when I pulled up, and I cursed under my breath for falling for Dinero's inconsistent bullshit. *His ass probably was here but got called away again*, I thought, rolling my eyes as I snatched up my work bag from the passenger seat and climbed out, now pissed that he'd thrown off my happiness.

I fumbled with my keys, looking for the one to my door, when car doors slamming behind me caught my attention and I jumped into defense mode. Being a young woman living alone, I was always on high alert when I was out at night. I tucked my keys between my fingers prepared to fight, but visibly relaxed when I saw it was just two police officers exiting their car. That was until they started up my walkway. Immediately, I tightened my hold on my bag as they approached me and tried to seem non-threatening.

"Can I help you, Officers?" I shrilled, unable to keep the nervousness out of my voice because both of their expressions were grim as fuck. One was sloppy bodied and looked like he had no business patrolling the streets, while the other one looked like one of the cops I'd seen on Instagram. He was only a little taller than me and built, filling out his uniform to the point that it seemed one deep breath away from tearing off his body. I put my focus on him as they got closer, hoping that looking at a fine ass policeman would ease my worry.

"Maam? Are you Ca'Mahri Harris?" the fat one huffed, adjusting his holster.

"Yes, that's me, but—"

"You're under arrest for the assault and battery of a Britney Cole. Can you put your arms behind your back?" he continued, reaching out for me, and I instantly took a step back.

"Hold up! I don't even know a damn Britney! Y'all got the wrong person!" When fat man couldn't get his hands on me, I realized what the more fit officer was for, as he made light work of grabbing me and removing my bag so he could slap the cuffs on my ass. I was still going off and struggling with them as I was read my rights and led to the squad car, trying to figure out who the fuck Britney Cole was. "Can y'all at least get my bag?" I shouted since they had left it in the middle of the sidewalk like I didn't have anything worth stealing in there.

"In a min—"

"Aye, why the fuck y'all handlin' her like that?" Dinero

appeared out of nowhere and started going off on them about any and everything. With him there asking questions, they switched roles once again and the buff one approached him trying to explain, while I was tucked into the backseat of their car. He was talking lowly, so I couldn't hear what he was saying, but whatever it was had Dinero pissed off. His crazy ass shoulder checked the officer and went to grab my bag. "I'm gone meet you at the station, baby, don't even trip!" he shouted before walking off.

True to his word, he pulled up to the precinct right behind us and followed behind the officer that was holding me, talking shit the whole time. I would've thought that he'd calm down some once we got to the station, but Dinero didn't give a single fuck about being outnumbered. That made me feel a little better knowing he was there and was going to get me right out. At the most I'd be sitting for an hour, and then I'd be free to find out what they thought I did.

The handsome officer ended up taking me to the holding cell, and I found out that his name was Walker since every cop we passed wanted to speak to him like some damn groupies. I was thankful as hell that besides me there were only two other women in the cell; one standing at the bars that looked like she was a damn runaway, and the other was sitting on the bench with her head tucked in her lap. As soon as the gate closed behind me, though, she popped her head up and I realized it was my damn sister!

"Camille, what the fuck you doin' here?" I gasped as she jumped to her feet with her face balled up. No wonder her ass hadn't answered her phone.

"*We're* here because Walt's stupid ass baby mamas some scary ass hoes!" Fuming, she began to pace the small area while realization kicked in. Our fight at the club had definitely been the only battery I could think of, but I didn't even know that bitch's name so I was completely thrown off. I would have put up more of a fight if I had known I was being locked up because of them, especially considering that they'd approached us on some bullshit! "I know that lame ass nigga told them hoes our information, and I can't wait to tell Cash's crazy ass! He better fuck him up too!"

"Camille, don't be sayin' shit like that all loud. They'll fuck around and charge you with threats," I scoffed, already over the whole situation. This wasn't the first time that we'd found ourselves behind bars together for some rowdy shit, because we definitely had a wild streak in our younger years. The difference now, though, was that we were grown and the bitches had decided to press charges. Now I wished I had gone even harder at the club because at least then I'd feel like it was worth it.

"Tuh! That ain't no threat, it's definitely a promise! Stupid ass bitches!" her crazy ass continued to ramble as she walked, and the girl in the corner snickered.

"Excuse me, can you let the guy out there know that my sister will need her bond paid too?" I called out to the nearest officer who happened to be walking by. His ass barely looked up at me and I groaned in aggravation. "Hello! Can you tell my boyfriend that we need two bonds! He's up there now, his name is Dinero Banks!" That seemed to catch his attention, and he paused.

"Dinero Banks is your boyfriend?" he asked for clarification, and I nodded vigorously.

"Yes, yes! He's right up front about to pay my bond, I need him to know my sister's back here too," I told him urgently, finally feeling like I was getting somewhere when he walked off with a stiff nod.

Whatever the officer said, we were being called for release a half hour later and by the time we made it up front, Cash had arrived too. Just like his crazy ass girl, he was going off and making threats, trying to find out which officer had brought her in despite me and Dinero trying to calm him down. We eventually got him to leave, only because Camille's messy ass brought up the fact that Walt had to be the reason the baby mamas knew our names and addresses, which turned his rage onto the trio. Once we got outside, me and my sister hugged before she slid into Cash's car, and I got into Dinero's. The guys stood outside talking for a few minutes before separating and as soon as Dinero got behind the wheel, he placed a hand on my thigh.

"You good?" he asked, looking at me with a raised brow, and I just nodded silently. At the moment I was relieved to be out of lockup, but I knew that this was far from the end. We would still need to go to court, and I could only hope that they didn't decide to follow through with the charges, because I didn't need anything affecting my chances of obtaining my RN.

CHAPTER SIXTEEN

DINERO

Ca'Mahri had been down since I'd bonded her out, and I quickly found out it was because the charges could fuck up her plans of going back to school, which pissed me off. Mostly, because I'd seen the shit go down and knew that the girls she and Camille had beat up had approached them, but also because I didn't play police games. Walt's baby mamas would've gotten more respect if they had tried to get another fair one, but they'd gone out of their way to press charges, and his lame ass had given them the information they needed to do so. Unfortunately, he'd been MIA since popping up with the nigga Lox a couple weeks back. Cash was on a mission to find his ass, though, and had already put out the word that he wanted him and his baby mamas' whereabouts.

I was trying to take a different route and just pay a lawyer to shut their shit down, but whatever worked out in the girls' favor was fine with me. Shit between us already had been shaky, but the added stress of a pending court case only made her ass more distant. I had been trying to spare some time for her considering the shit I had going on myself, but it wasn't proving to be an easy task. In addition to my regular day-to-day schedule, my pops had insisted that we move the trap after we told him about the shit with Lox, and that shit was taking a while. We had a lot of shit to consider when moving, so it was shut down until we had it all figured out, which stopped that source of income. It had been a couple of weeks already and the two hundred thousand that we were out was already being missed.

"Get yo' head out yo' ass, boy, we got a drop to get ready for." Cash breezed into my office at the funeral home in a full hazmat suit, and I had to do a double take.

"Nigga, what the fuck you got on?" I quizzed, and this nigga looked down at his clothes with a frown.

"It's protective gear so I don't fuck up my clothes doin' this shit! I don't even know why that nigga Jose wanna do shit like this anyway instead of just using the cars like everybody else," he grumbled, dropping into the chair across from me.

"Because it's easier for him to move bodies than cars, ole pussy ass nigga. You barely have to even touch anything, so quit whining."

"Naw, 'cause Ramone's ass mixed the bodies up last time and embalmed one of them muhfuckas, and the shit got all over my damn Gucci sweater!" he scoffed, shaking his head. "That shit ain't happening again, that's why you need to hire somebody else to help his old ass out down there."

"Or maybe yo' ass just don't need to be wearin' Gucci when we're working in here."

"Obviously, I know that now, goofy ass nigga!" I shook my head as I climbed out of my chair and removed my watch and chains, placing them in the drawer. Unlike Cash, I knew better than to wear anything of value in the basement of our funeral home. It was too much of a risk with the type of shit we had down there, so I didn't even take any chances on that shit.

He followed me out of the office, still talking shit as we made our way down the stairs to the basement, where we had a trap door for our illegal dealings. I hit the thermostat on the wall, revealing a number pad, and punched in the code, making the brick wall slide apart.

"Yo' ass swears you James Bond or some shit." Cash chuckled from beside me like this was his first time seeing me do the shit. I flipped his ass the finger and stepped into the room on the other side where Ramone was shuffling back and forth loading packs of cocaine into the corpse on the first table. Slipping on a pair of gloves, I followed suit and started on the next while Cash went to the third. With the three of us working, it didn't take long for us to finish stuffing the bodies and stapling them up for transport. We wheeled them through the connected garage and placed them into a hearse that Jose had one of his men driving in exchange for two duffle bags of money, and after checking to make sure it was all there, the man was on his way. I had to admit that the funeral home was some of the easiest money we made, considering that all we had to do was pay the coroner for some of their John Does, stuff them, and send them off. I wished all of our shit was that easy.

"You do the count and lock up today, nigga, I got some shit to do," I told Cash as he stepped out of his hazmat right there in the garage, and he instantly paused, looking up at me with his forehead bunched.

"How you know I ain't got some shit to do?"

"Yo' ass always doin' somethin'. Sit yo' ass still and do some work, I already been pickin' up yo' slack since you met Camille, ole' soft-hearted ass nigga." That had his face twisting in even more of a scowl, but he knew he couldn't argue facts.

I'd really been letting him skate with a lot of shit and had just been taking care of everything on my own, but obviously, I needed to chill on that. It was making him think that he didn't have to do as much, and that wasn't the case. If his ass was going to be getting paid half, then he needed to do half the work, fuck that other shit.

"You lucky shorty at work and Maria got Kash, ugly ass boy," he grumbled, finally discarding the suit and lifting both bags of money.

"Naw, you lucky Camille ain't found out that Maria yo' in-house pussy! Keep playin' and I'ma tell her lil' crazy ass!"

"Man, fuck you! I ain't touched that girl in a minute," he complained, trudging behind me as I made my way back inside. I believed him because he had definitely switched shit up for Camille, but the thing with women was that it wouldn't matter when the last time he'd hit was. The fact that another female was still around that he'd been fucking was enough of a violation in their eyes, but I wasn't goin to tell his smart ass shit.

"Better fire her ass then." I shrugged.

"Nigga, for what? She been there for years and she do good work," he quizzed as we got back to my office, and I washed my hands before putting my jewelry back on. His ass was really standing there looking puzzled, but I was on a mission and didn't have time to explain the shit to him.

"Ask Pops, man, I'm out." I left him there still confused as hell and headed out to my car. Ca'Mahri's last day at her job was the night before, and I had plans to finally take her out. I'd called in a favor earlier that day knowing that she was going to be free, and I hoped her ass liked it because I had put a lot of thought into that shit. Pulling up to her crib, I parked behind her car and went up to her door.

She answered with her face frowned up until she saw it

was me. Before she could even get the smart shit she was thinking out of her mouth, I dropped a quick kiss on her lips. Her fine ass was dressed in a tie-dye graphic tee and some black leggings, but easily made it look sexy. That's how I knew I was feeling her for real, because it didn't matter what she was wearing I thought her ass looked good, and it didn't matter if she called herself having an attitude, I still wanted to be around her. I definitely hadn't felt that way about a woman since Tania, so I knew her little mean ass had worked her way into my chest.

"Dinero," she hummed, stepping back so I could come inside, but I pulled her back against me and leaned down close to her face.

"*Ca'Mahri*," I mocked. "I freed up my day so we could finally share that meal I been promising you. Now gone get yo' shoes on." Her face instantly lit up in surprise, and she melted into me with a smile.

"The whole day?" She raised her brow, and I nodded. "No runnin' away after a phone call?"

"I'ma cut this muhfucka off. Thug's honor," I promised with a hand over my heart, making her roll her eyes, but she still ran off to grab her shoes.

When we made it to Navy Pier a short time later, there was a bunch of disgruntled people walking back to their cars or wherever they'd come from, as we walked to the entrance with our hands locked.

"Where they all goin'?" she questioned, beginning to drag her feet, but I pulled her back into my side, this time holding her by the waist.

"They're leavin' 'cause the pier closed to everybody but us for the next two hours," I bragged, flashing her a toothy grin. She argued with me the entire way to the entrance until she saw my guy Tony still turning people away as he let us in. Since

I'd met her mean ass I hadn't seen her smile so much as when she realized we had free range of the whole thing. She had me running through there like a big ass kid, riding the centennial wheel and going into the funhouses. We even got to take out one of the tour boats for a half hour before ending the night with a go-kart ride on the waterfront.

Just like I'd hoped, Ca'Mahri enjoyed all of that childish ass shit, but I couldn't front like I didn't have fun playing around too. The only time I ever got to do some shit like that was when I was out with the family for Kash since he was so little, but I knew that it wouldn't be my last, especially if Ca'Mahri had anything to do with it. She was so tired that her ass was snoring by the time we got in the car, so instead of driving her home or driving out to Winnekta, I headed a few blocks over to my apartment.

"Aye, wake yo' sleepy ass up." I roused her once we made it into the parking garage. She sat up, wiping the slob away from her chin, and I coughed to cover up the laugh that was ready to erupt from how lost she looked. It didn't make sense how easily she fell into a deep sleep.

"I'm up," she grunted huskily, finally taking in her surroundings with narrowed eyes. "Where we at?"

"We at my crib, girl, come on." I helped her out of the low bucket seats, and we walked to the elevator with her head tucked against my arm. It was still pretty early by city standards, so there were a few people on with us, some I'd seen before in passing and one I knew for a fact I'd hit before. I stood next to the control panel and pulled Ca'Mahri's body in front of mine, hoping the girl didn't say anything stupid in front of her. Thankfully, she remained silent, aside from staring a hole in my face, and soon she was stepping off behind some stiff ass nigga in a suit.

Shaking my head, I put my focus back on my shorty since

by now she was all the way up and on her clingy shit. With her head against my chest, the sweet smell of her hair filled my nostrils. She'd gotten rid of the braids and was now wearing her natural hair in a ball on top of her head that damn near blocked my view it was so big. I was realizing that baby girl didn't like to keep hairstyles for too long, but from what I knew of women and beauty salons, she had to have a plug to get in as often as she did.

"Damn, what floor you live on?" she joked after we were the only ones left on the elevator, and I laughed, nodding at the overhead panel.

"This one." She seemed surprised when we landed at the penthouse, and kept looking between me and the open doors like she didn't know if she should step through. "Gone head." With my hands stuffed into my hoodie pockets, I watched her walk from room to room in awe. She finally ended up at the window walls that surrounded the living room and was staring out over the city. I could admit that the view was definitely breathtaking. In fact, it was the main reason I'd even decided on having such an exclusive ass apartment, because I didn't like spending on unnecessary shit. I felt like I deserved that view, though, and figured if worse came to worse, I could always rent it out and have a passive income.

"All this time I been thinkin' yo' ass is hood rich, but between this place and the one we went to in Winnekta, nigga, you rich, rich," she said, tilting her head once I came over and hugged her from behind. "What you want with an everyday ass hood chick, like me? I mean, I'm a CNA, me and you together ain't no damn power couple." I didn't like how she sounded so down about what she had compared to what I had. Ambition and hard work were just as valuable to me as a girl who came with money, because I knew with those skills she could *make* money. Sighing, I turned her around so I could look into her face, immediately seeing the uneasiness there.

"What wouldn't a nigga want with you? You're smart and hardworking, unlike some of these leechin' ass hoes that had shit handed to them their whole lives. You keep shit real with me and hold my ass accountable, even when you know it's gone piss me off." I cupped her face and rubbed my thumb across her cheek, and she simpered from my touch. "Shit, you're the whole package in my eyes and as far as that power couple shit, who says we can't be? You're already furthering your education, and shit, nursing is the wave right now. Plus, if shit don't work out wherever you choose to flex yo' skill, havin' a nurse on the payroll ain't a bad idea." I shrugged, finally making her release a small smile. I had meant all that shit, though, and I was realizing that I had fucked around and got caught up. A nigga hadn't said it yet, but I knew the feeling I was getting in my chest when it came to Ca'Mahri. It was one I'd been running from for years and she'd managed to put a stop to all that in a matter of a couple months. *I was in love, damn.*

CHAPTER SEVENTEEN
CAMILLE

"So, you're knockin' having a baby mama off your checklist?" Noelle's nosy ass asked, leaning over the small table like that little bit of tea would quench her thirst. I wasn't ready to admit out loud that I had fallen victim to a baby daddy, but considering that I was well acquainted with that nigga's son, then I guess that's what had happened. Ever since that first day I'd met him and he realized I knew his daddy, he stayed asking for me. At first I tried to keep what me and Cash had separate to some degree, but there was no denying that Kash had me wrapped around his little finger already. I was noticing shit that I never paid any attention to before, like Hot Wheels cars and little action figure men. If I was in the mall, I was snatching up a pair of shoes or a cute outfit for him too. The shit was crazy, but I couldn't stop myself. It seemed like in just a couple of months, me and Ca'Mahri had switched places, except I still didn't know if the nigga attached to the kid wasn't shit or not. Sure, Cash talked a good game and seemed like the total package, but a part of me still felt like some serious shit would happen soon that revealed that he was just like the rest. Since my heart couldn't take the possibility, I was keeping the last little bit of hoe in my back pocket just in case. I just hoped that I didn't kill his ass if I found anything out, because after so many heart breaks, it was a chance that I'd snap for real.

Shrugging, I took a sip of my bottled water. "Technically, I didn't knock nothin' off my list. That bitch been MIA since I met Cash, on some deadbeat shit," I said, making Noelle's eyes bug out of her head.

"You don't think he, *you know*?" she slid her thumb across her neck to symbolize killing, and I almost spit my water out. I wasn't naïve enough not to know what type of shit Cash was into, but despite his street ties, I didn't think any sane nigga would kill their damn baby mama for just giving up her duties.

"What? Girl, hell naw! Yo' ass readin' too many hood romances!" I waved her off. "What's been up with you and Russ, while you all in my damn business?" Now it was her turn to scoff, and I couldn't hide my surprise. As far as I knew, they'd been as thick as thieves since meeting in the club a couple of months ago, and this was the first I was hearing her say anything bad about him.

"Fuck him! I see why his ass was the only single one out there that night." She sucked her teeth. "His ass got baby mama drama! I'm surprised one of them hoes didn't jump out the bushes on us the night we met!"

"One of? Damn, how many he got?"

"Four baby mamas and six damn kids!" she told me, and now I understood why she'd been all in my damn business. I wouldn't have wanted to think about the type of drama they were bringing either. "I really oughta curse Dinero's ass out for not warning me."

"Like you would've listened to him. Yo' ass was drunk and tryna salvage the night." I chuckled, even as I felt my anger rising just thinking about how Walt's baby mama posse had started some shit that night.

"True. What they sayin' about y'all's case though?"

"Tuh, just that those bitches wanna continue to pursue charges. If I catch them or Walt's bum ass anywhere, though, it's gone go up! I don't care if they're in the prayer line at church, they're gonna catch this action for that hoe shit!"

"Not in church, sis."

"Yep, church! Hell, I might even do it in court! Let me stop, I definitely ain't fighting nobody in court."

"Facts! Don't be out here fuckin' up yo' livelihood for nobody!" she said, and I had to give her a high-five. I talked a lot of shit and would no doubt back it up, but I wasn't trying to fuck up my good name for no bitch.

Before I knew it, our lunch break was coming to an end, and we hurried to clear off the table. By the time we went to walk out, Ca'Mahri was finally walking in, looking pissed off, and I didn't even have to ask why. Ever since Reyna had found out that she was my sister, she had been giving her the same amount of issues that she'd given me.

"Dang, you're just now gettin' lunch?" I frowned, and she smacked her lips.

"Yeah, man, *Reyna* been on my ass all day and even when I told her me and Glenda were supposed to be trading so I could have lunch with y'all, she told me we couldn't do that." She made a face as she mocked the voice that Reyna had used.

"Well, that's where you fucked up at. Don't ever say you goin' to lunch with us to Reyna's hatin' ass. She already on her bullshit with you 'cause you my sister," I grumbled, and Noelle nodded in agreement. Everybody around there knew Reyna didn't like cliques and she really didn't like my ass.

"I wish y'all hoes would've said somethin' before I took the job, thinkin' I was gone be able to hang with y'all. Now I gotta eat by myself," she complained and had the nerve to pout like a big ass baby.

"Girl, you'll be okay. Tomorrow we'll make sure we all go together, even if I gotta come get you myself." The promise did little to stop her moping, but she did go ahead and get in the line for food, grumbling under her breath the whole time. Noelle and I went our separate ways next since the doctor had been giving out lab requests like he was Oprah or some shit. Literally, from the time I clocked back in from lunch to the time I officially clocked out at three, I was running around doing patients left and right. I was relieved as hell to finally be leaving that damn jungle. Usually, I would've been going straight home so I could at least shower and change my clothes before I went to Cash's house, but I wasn't in the mood for that much driving. He'd been insisting on me going over there or him coming to my crib whenever we both had free time, unless he told me otherwise, and since he hadn't said anything yet, I was headed to his house. His clothes were definitely more comfortable to chill in, or maybe it was just me falling right into the role of being somebody's girlfriend despite my constant denials.

I rolled my eyes when my phone went off with a call from him, even though I couldn't deny the way my heart leapt seeing that nigga's name. It was like he always knew when he was on my mind, with his crazy ass. I allowed the handsfree to answer, and his deep voice came blaring through my cars speaker, sounding sexy as hell.

"Where you at, you already on yo' way to the crib?" he asked, and I could hear Dinero yelling in the background, so I cut down the volume a bit.

"You sound thirsty, nigga. I'm in traffic, bouta head out to this dice game."

"Ahhh, you got jokes! You better quit playin' and take yo'

ass to the crib, and when I get there you better be in the bed booty hole naked too!" he demanded, making me bust out laughing.

"You the one with jokes! It feel like go have a drink with yo' girls out here, and you ain't even in the house yet anyway. Why I gotta rush?" I continued fucking with him, knowing damn well I wasn't in the mood to do shit but kick my feet up and watch TV, preferably with him.

"Maaan, cut it out, Camille." His voice turned serious, and I knew that if we were on FaceTime he would've been giving me his stern face. Shit, he was probably already making the face even though I couldn't see it.

"Ahhh, look at you gettin' all mad, I was just playin'. I'm drivin' to the house now, crybaby." The fact that he wanted me at his house while he wasn't home was like a double-edged sword, because with a man like Cash, it meant something when they invited you into their home and around their kids without supervision. On the other hand, though, I'd dealt with niggas that only wanted to pinpoint your location so you wouldn't catch them doing dirt. Although I was trying to put my suspicious side to rest, it was almost engrained in me now and I had to resist the urge to say something smart.

"Riiiight, 'cause you already know," he bragged, like he had done something, and I rolled my eyes. "If Kash not there with Maria, then make sure you set that pussy out for me." The mention of his raggedy ass maid instantly put me in a bad mood. I'd found out that she was the one who'd been looking all upside my head at his parents' party that day and ever since, I'd had a bad taste in my mouth about her ass. She was smart enough to play cordial whenever Cash or any of his family was around, but I didn't like her vibe at all. It was to the point that I felt like she was on some Lifetime movie shit and would try to kill my ass, but we both knew she was smarter than that. She was another one of the many things I was giving Cash the benefit of doubt with, because there was no way he was crazy enough to have that bitch in my face if he'd fucked with her like that. At least that was what I was telling myself anyway.

"I *hope* that weird bitch ain't there," I grumbled, pulling up to the gate just as Keshia's silver Benz was coming out. She waved and blew her horn as we passed each other, and I sent up a silent prayer that Kash was in the car or at least in her house with Kendrick and not with Maria, even though I knew that was wishful thinking. I'd been so caught up in my thoughts I'd missed whatever Cash was saying in my ear in defense of that bitch. "Okay, I made it. Don't have me waiting long either, Cash." I hung up without giving him a chance to say anything else because he'd already blown me in that quick ass phone call.

Walking in the house, I listened out for any sound of Kash or Maria and called out for them when I was met with silence. "Maria! Kash!" That shit echoed right back to me and I shrugged, happy that her ass wasn't there. Since we'd be the only ones home, Cash could definitely make shit up to me by kissing my ass, literally, and I was going to lay in his bed naked until he got there too. After slipping out of my shoes, I switched to the laundry room on the first floor and stripped naked right there, throwing my clothes in the wash before heading upstairs where Cash's multiple shower heads were waiting on me. Aside from the whirlpool tub, the shower was the best part of the house for me because it always felt like a million little fingers massaging my skin.

I stepped in after adjusting the water to my liking and instantly let out a satisfied moan from a mixture of hot water and the way it felt hitting my skin. I stood in there for over thirty minutes before finally reaching for my bodywash.

Another fifteen minutes later, I was all clean and smelling edible. Cutting the water off, I wrapped one of his thick gray towels around my body and shuffled barefoot into his room. That shower had me so sleepy that I could barely keep my eyes open as I rubbed my bum bum cream that I kept there on my skin, and by the time I'd actually finished, I didn't even feel like going through the drawers for something of Cash's to sleep in. His freaky ass had told me to be naked anyway, so that's just what I was when I crawled up to the head of his bed and slipped underneath the sheets. I hadn't even intended on going to sleep when I got there, but I figured a quick nap wouldn't hurt as my eyelids drooped closed.

"Ahhhh, baaaby!" I woke up cumming, with my legs spread apart while Cash did figure eights in my pussy. The room was dark, letting me know that I'd slept much longer than I planned to, but with Cash smacking on my juices, I couldn't even think about that. He always had me in a trance when he went to work, and I could count on having multiple orgasms every time. "Ooooh, fuck, I'm bouta cum again, Cash, shiiiit!" I reached down to caress his head as I orgasmed, only to come up with a handful of fucking hair. Instinctively, I yanked that shit, causing a very feminine ass yelp in reply, and I blacked clean the fuck out.

CHAPTER EIGHTEEN
CASH

The last fucking thing I was expecting when I walked in my bedroom was for a naked ass brawl to be going on. When I first came through the door and heard all the commotion, I thought for sure somebody was robbing my ass, so I took the safety off my gun and ran up the stairs two at a time, only to find Camille's bare ass in the air as she pummeled a half-naked Maria. For a second, the sight had me just standing there frozen, but the sound of Maria's screams for help quickly snapped me out of my trance.

"Yoooo, what the fuck goin' on in here!" I was so damn discombobulated I didn't know what to ask first, I just immediately went into action and tucked my gun in my waist before snatching Camille up. Her crazy ass was still swinging and letting out animalistic grunts as she tried to get to Maria, who was now sitting up and holding her bloody face in her hands.

"I told you this bitch was crazy! I woke up to her eating my damn pussy!"

"Whaaaat thhhhe fuuuuck?" A nigga was really confused as hell. Not really that Maria ate pussy, because there'd been a couple of times that we'd taken bitches down together, but more so because she acted like she hated Camille's ass.

"Let me go! I'm bouta rip that bitch head from her neck like a Barbie doll!" Camille snapped, sounding like her ass was possessed by the devil.

"Lo siento! I thought she was like the others, Papi!" Maria cried, attempting to stop her bleeding with the shirt she had on.

"Others!" Camille exploded, and I swear I felt her damn near vibrating. Now it was obvious what that bitch was doing, because she knew damn well Camille wasn't shit like the hoes I brought home. Immediately, Dinero's words popped into my head, and I released a heavy sigh. That was all the distraction Camille's crazy ass needed, and she did some self-defense shit and elbowed my ass in the lip. Hearing Maria's confession had her turning her rage onto me.

"Baby, let me explain! It's not even like that!" My soft ass was damn near ready to beg for her to hear me out.

"No! I tried to hear yo' ass out and you lied, muhfucka! Now look, I done fucked this simple bitch up! I told you, *I told you*! Don't play with me, Cash! This is the shit that happens, when I get my feelings involved with niggas and they lie!" I could hear how hurt she was in her voice, but tough ass Camille wasn't going to let me see not one tear. She was already pacing, which I'd learned early on was what she did when she was too mad to calm herself down. Seeing her so pissed off, made me realize how simple it would've been if I had just told the truth, or at the least gotten rid of Maria's ass.

"Ayite, I admit it was fucked up to not tell you, but I didn't lie, Camille, and you know that shit!" I grumbled, touching my lip and growing annoyed at the sight of blood. "I oughta fuck yo' ass up for putting yo' hands on me, bruh. I don't like that shit."

"Ohhhh, you don't like that shit, huh? Well, I don't like waking up to bitches mouth raping me! How would you feel if that was you, tuh! Yo' ass would probably like that nutty shit! You and her and yo' missing baby mama can have this shit!" She waved me off and snatched up her towel from the bed like she was about to leave, but I grabbed her around the waist to stop her while Maria's simple ass watched us with wide eyes.

"What the fuck you still doin' sittin' there! Yo' ass fuckin' fired, ole big mouth ass!" I roared, still wrestling around with Camille's strong ass. I swear if her shit opened any bigger, they'd be falling out into her lap. She obviously didn't think that losing her job was an option, but she should've weighed the pros and cons of what she'd done. "Get the fuck out!"

"Naw, you don't gotta leave. I'll go, girl!" Once again, Maria looked between the two of us as if she wasn't sure who to listen to, and I realized just how dumb she actually was. Her lack of intellect didn't stop me from jumping in her direction with a growl, and she hurriedly scrambled out of the room, finally leaving us alone.

"Camille, listen, I know you're mad, but just tell me what to do I'll—"

"You could get the fuck out my face," she hummed, cocking her head to the side aggressively. Sighing, I stepped back and ran a hand down my face like that shit would wake me the fuck up out the twilight zone. Unfortunately, when I opened my eyes, Camille was still giving me a deadly look.

"Look, I don't even wanna fight. I just want you to put some clothes on and I'll let you leave—"

"Let me! Nigga, you gon' move the fuck out my way or—!"

"Camille!" I barked so loud that she jumped and instantly snapped her mouth shut. With her finally quiet, I lowered my voice, saying the rest a little more gently. "Just put some fuckin' clothes on." The look in my eyes must have told her not to test me, because she merely sucked her teeth and stomped into my closet, coming out a second later with the first thing she must have laid her eyes on, which was a white tee and some black joggers. She dramatically stuffed her limbs into the oversized clothes and once she finished, she threw her arms out with a huff.

"Happy?"

Silently, I stepped away from the door so she could pass and as soon as she was close enough, I reached out, grabbing her forearm. "Don't get comfortable, Camille," I said, staring into her eyes so she knew I was serious. She was mad now, and I was willing to give her time to cool off because I was wrong, but she was going to bring her ass back. The underlying threat had her swallowing hard as tears that she refused to let fall glistened in her eyes, before she snatched away and left. As soon as the front door slammed behind her, I punched a hole in the wall.

"Fuck!"

* * *

"You cool?" Dinero asked, and I looked at his ass like he was stupid. "Aye, I'm just askin', nigga. I been callin' yo' ass for like five minutes 'cause this yo' fifth time countin' that stack." He tossed his hands up and gestured to the stack of money in front of me, and I sighed heavily. It had only been a week since Camille left my crib, and she was on my mind heavily. I'd been trying to call her, but her sneaky ass blocked me, and not only that, she'd been staying at her parents' house in an effort to shake my ass. I had known that's where she was since the night she showed up, but the only reason I hadn't gone over there clowning was because I didn't want to disrespect her people's crib. She was smart enough to know I wouldn't do no stupid shit at her job either, so she'd been staying inside and only leaving to go to work. I'd thought about some of everything to get on her good side, including blowing Maria's shit back, but eventually decided against that. It'd be just my luck she used that as an excuse to stay mad at me on some reverse psychology shit.

The main thing that was fucking me up was the fact that Dinero's stupid ass had just told me to tell her what was up or fire that bitch, and I hadn't done either. His ass hadn't even said I told you so yet, which was surprising as fuck because he loved being right about some shit, but looking across the table, I didn't see shit but concern in his eyes.

"My bad, my head was on some other shit," I grumbled, reaching for the stack so I could make sure the count was right before moving on.

"Look, just give her a minute. Technically, she didn't just deal with your deceit that night, she was also violated." He leaned over like it was more than just us two in the room and said. I understood all of that, but I didn't like that running shit she was doing. It was like her defense mechanism because she'd been running from a nigga since I'd met her. I was trying to be the bigger person because I knew I was wrong, but it was getting to the point that I was starting to get pissed off. True, I had omitted that I fucked Maria before, but I'd never denied it and I damn sure ain't think her freak ass would hop in the bed with her either. A lot of the shit wasn't really my fault, but I was the only one being punished out of the whole situation. I tried to keep my face neutral as I nodded like I was taking in everything he said, even though the truth was that soon, I was going to bring her ass back whether she was ready or not. His talkative ass was still running his mouth when my phone started ringing. Seeing Vernique's name, I immediately declined that shit and did the same thing when she called back a few seconds later. I wasn't in the headspace to talk to her ass and would probably be ready to send a hitter after her if she said the wrong thing.

I shook off all of the outside distractions and zoned in on the task at hand so I could get that shit over with quickly and go pick up Kash from my OG. Since it wasn't much left, we were finished in less than a half hour, and I stood up stretching while Dinero's soft ass took a call from Ca'Mahri and loaded the money back in the bags.

"Aye, you good to drop this shit off?" he asked, looking like he was ready to sprint up out of there when he finally hung up.

"Man, stop askin' me that shit! You actin' like I'm on suicide watch or somethin'!" He stared at me for a second like that was really what he was worried about and let out a low whistle.

"Shiiiit, I don't know, nigga. The way you mopin' around, you might need to be."

"I'm good, ole goofy ass nigga!" I fumed, snatching the fully stuffed bag and zipping it up so I could leave. His irritating ass laughed behind me as I went out to my car, leaving him to lock up.

By the time I pulled through the gate at home and stopped in front of my parents' house, it was barely after nine p.m. and with all the lights they had on, I knew Kash's little ass was up and causing hell. He'd been a great distraction from the shit going on, but eventually he was going to get tired of my clingy ass and probably already was. When I let myself in the door, all I could hear was that damn baby shark song playing loud as hell, and I shook my head. My mama let that nigga get away with anything. I wasn't even surprised to see her in the vast living room, doing that stupid ass dance with him, but what did have my forehead scrunched up was my pops right there with them hitting every move. Since neither had noticed me, I pulled my phone out and started recording their grown asses in their pajamas dancing like nobody was watching.

"Yooooo, wait till I tell niggas, Dolla up in here baby sharkin'!" I let my presence be known, cracking up, and my pops instantly looked like a deer in headlights before his face hardened and he raised his middle finger at me. "Aye yo, that ain't a family friendly gesture, nigga!" Waving me off, he went to sit down while Kash decided to try and show me the dance.

"Cash, leave my baby alone, he's on grandpa duties and here you come cracking jokes!" my mama fussed, sounding out of breath as fuck as she took a seat beside him on the cream-colored loveseat.

"Maaan, y'all bouta go viral, fuck all that!"

"Boy—!" My pops went to jump up, but my mama held him back, wrapping herself around his arm and patting his chest like he was Bane or some shit.

"It's okay, baby. Can you help Kash get ready to go while I talk to him quick?" she said sweetly before whispering something in his ear that had his old ass grinning. Giving her a quick kiss, he ushered Kash out of the room, jumping at me as they passed. My mama wasted no time patting the seat next to her, and I sighed but went and sat down. I already knew she was about to talk her shit, but I really wasn't trying to hear it from her ass too.

Whap!

"Damn, Ma! What the fuck!"

As soon as my ass landed on the cushion, she smacked the back of my head hard as hell and gave me a stern look. "Didn't I tell yo' silly ass about that hoe livin' over there?"

"Yeah, but—"

"No buts, you fucked up, so you fix it and get my damn daughter-in-law back," she ordered.

"Maaan, you barely knew shorty for a month!" I scoffed,

still rubbing the sore spot on my head. It seemed like every-body had already picked a side, and it was definitely Camille's. Shrugging, she stood up.

"So, I'm yo' mama, I know when somebody good for you." Her simple words were cut off by my pops and Kash entering the room with his shoes and hoodie on. Done with her spiel, she put her focus on giving him a couple hugs and kisses before sending our asses out.

CHAPTER NINETEEN
CA'MAHRI

I had a lot on my plate with work, school, and my blossoming relationship with Dinero, but I was managing to juggle it all surprisingly well. Despite our schedules conflicting a lot, we were still able to make time for each other, and most of the time he was encouraging me to do my work or helping me to study. I'd never had that before outside of my family. I was used to niggas not thinking that school was as important as your hustle, because the future was limited to the next day, or week, or month. Dinero was different, he was already asking me about my goals after school and what I wanted to do with my degree. That shit was sexy as hell, and only made me want to be under him even more, despite the shit that Cash had done. I didn't want to believe that he was capable of the same things but if I was being honest, the thought was gnawing at the back of my mind, thinking that he may have been too good to be true. It didn't help that Camille was now on a rampage and trying to shit on anything love or relationship related, just like she'd been before she met Cash.

It was one of the first days we'd all had off together and we decided to spend it with our parents since we barely were able to get together, but as soon as my mama pulled out the margaritas, my daddy had disappeared. He didn't play that drinking with his little girls shit, and he also knew the type of conversation that was going to happen once the liquor kicked in. Now we were sitting around the table working on our second drinks each and playing card games as we talked.

"I'm just sayin', you better keep an eye on that nigga, 'cause ain't no tellin' what he doin' over there with his live-ins," Camille pointed out with her face balled up, and Noelle nodded in agreement. Rolling my eyes, I took a sip of my drink and pulled a card from the deck, inspecting it briefly before setting it aside.

"Dinero doesn't have live-ins. He cleans up behind himself and when he can't, he calls a cleaning company," I said dryly, and they both looked stumped for a second before she went to try again and was quickly cut off by my mama.

"Camille, stop it. Dinero seems to be good for your sister, and unless he shows otherwise, then you need to be happy for them. You too, Noelle, with yo' cosigning ass." She looked between the two of them sternly.

"I'm just sayin', Ma, dang!"

"Well, just stop sayin' 'cause you're soundin' real bitter right about now." Camille's mouth dropped, and I held back a chuckle. No doubt her situation with Cash was unusual as hell and I definitely felt bad about it, but I didn't want her trying to put doubts in my mind about Dinero because she was mad at him at the moment. Unlike all of the other men she'd dealt with, I saw that she was really opening up with Cash and probably loved his ass, which was why she still kept in touch with his family. She thought I didn't know that shit, but Keshia had a big mouth and had already let it slip.

"I am not bitter *Allani*—!"

"Oh, these drinks too strong up in here if they got you callin' me by my damn name, girl!" My mama lifted up out of her chair and lunged at her, and we all fell out laughing.

"I'm just playin', Ma!" Camille threw her hands up, not wanting any smoke with our mama.

"That's what I thought, lil' girl!"

I was still laughing when I saw that Dinero was calling me and instantly, my stomach started swarming with butterflies. The nigga had me gone already and I hadn't even got the dick yet, which was crazy as hell to me. I figured he was waiting on the right time, but eventually, I was going to end up just taking it if he didn't make a move.

"Hey, baby," I cooed, and all eyes landed on me, so I turned away from their nosy asses to give us a little privacy.

"Oh, I'm baby now?" he teased, using my words on me, and I could hear the smile in his voice.

"You got jokes, huh?"

"Naw, I'm just fuckin' with you, but you still chillin' with yo' people?" The question had me looking back at the table, and all of them were tuned into my conversation but were playing it off like they weren't.

"Yessss,"

"Ohhhh, you a lil' tipsy, huh?" He chuckled, and I had to agree because I was. My mama was heavy handed with the tequila on the second round, and I was definitely feeling it.

"Just a lil'."

"Well, it's still kinda early, so hopefully you good by seven 'cause I got some shit planned for you. You think you'll be good by then?"

"Yeah, that's like five hours away," I scoffed, already planning how I was going to get out of not having any more drinks.

"Still gotta get dressed and do yo' hair and all that girly shit, so I don't know if that's gone be a lot of time with how long you take to get ready." Now I was really curious because he'd never really been worried about how long I took getting ready. Dinero was always full of surprises, though, so there was really no telling what he had planned, but I was excited, nonetheless.

"I'll be ready, sir," I groaned playfully.

"Ayite, your dress and everything is already at your house. I'ma see you in a few." He hung up before I could question him about what he meant and suddenly, I wanted to cut the day short just so I could go and see.

"Ohh, this heffa bouta dip on us, y'all!" Noelle was the first to speak when I turned back around to them, trying not to look so geeked.

"Really, Cam?"

"In a little bit, he's not comin' to get me til' seven so I can still sit for a while," I promised, making them grumble while my mama waved them off.

"Don't mind these lonely fools. Let that man spoil you, baby," she encouraged, patting my hand.

We spent the next couple of hours playing a few games and listening to music, and I quickly lost track of the time. When I finally looked up and realized it was going on six, I hopped up and told their asses goodbye. I would still need to shower and do my makeup before Dinero's punctual ass showed up. Speeding home, I made it in roughly fifteen minutes and hurried inside to find two bags from Saks on my bed, and it took everything in me to bypass it and head straight to the shower. I jumped in so quick that I didn't even wait until the water got warm, but I hurried to wash my body, before running a razor over my legs and squirting Palmer's oil all over my body. For sure, it was going to have me soft as hell. Patting dry, I wrapped my towel around my body and sat down on the edge of my bed while I rubbed on my Olay lotion and sprayed some Guilty Gucci on my pressure points.

By the time I finished with that, I only had about fifteen minutes left to get dressed. I took that time to look at what Dinero had bought for me so that I'd know if I should go all out with my makeup, and damn if my baby hadn't shown the fuck out. The strapless Monique Lhuillier dress had to be the most expensive pieces of clothing I'd ever held in my hands and felt extremely soft against my skin. It was covered in sequins and had a high split up the thigh that gave the dress a splash of feistiness. As soon as I saw it, I immediately knew how I was going to wear my hair and my makeup.

I quickly did a light beat, with a smokey eye and nude glossy lip, before smoothing my hair up into a high bun, and added a small gold clamp to add to the look. I kept my jewelry simple with just pair of diamond studs and a dainty gold necklace, since the dress itself was covered in sequins. When I finished, I stood in my bedroom mirror looking at myself in appreciation. The open-toed red bottoms had me looking grown, grown, and I already knew that would be the night. They had me feeling so damn sexy that I considered leaving them on when I finally threw the pussy at Dinero. The thought had barely crossed my mind, and I heard the door opening and closing behind him, suddenly making me nervous.

"Calm yo' ass down, bitch!" I chastised, taking a deep breath and heading out just as he reached the hallway.

We both paused, taking each other in lustfully. Dinero always gave upper echelon vibes, but in the black-on-black tailormade suit, with a silk tie and shirt underneath, he looked like a CEO. *My CEO*. Shuddering, I had to tell myself not to lure his fine ass in the room and say fuck whatever he had planned, especially with the way he was looking at me.

"Damn, baby." Licking his lips, he rubbed his hands

together and pulled me in for a kiss. "Let's hurry up and get up outta here before I fuck around and cancel this shit." I simpered as he grabbed my hand and led me out of there, locking the door behind us. Outside there was an awaiting town car, and the driver stood with the door open waiting on us to get in.

"Ooooh, fancy," I teased as we climbed inside, and he just shrugged.

"Oh, this ain't shit, watch me work." He popped the cork on a bottle of champagne and handed me a glass before pouring one for himself. *Oh, he's definitely getting some pussy!*

I still didn't have a clue where we were going and was confused as hell when we pulled up to the airport, right on the tarmac next to the huge ass planes. I damn near choked once we stopped and the driver came to open the door again. Turning to Dinero with wide eyes, I found him chuckling.

"Gone head, baby, you good." He nodded, gesturing for me to take the man's hand and step out. He came out right behind me and shook the man's hand before wrapping his arm around me and walking me over to a smaller plane that had its stairs out and the staff standing there waiting.

"Nooo, Dinero!" I tried to pull away in complete disbelief. "No! Stop fuckin' playin' with me right now!"

"Girl, if you don't bring yo' ass on, we already got a long ride ahead of us." I had only been on a plane a handful of times, and they were all overrun with loud babies and rude people. This was clearly going to be a different experience, and I was pulling him along at this point. I took my time climbing the steps onto the aircraft as the flight attendants all greeted us and led us to the seating area. Everything was covered in a light cream color with mahogany trim and looked almost too expensive to touch. The fact that I didn't have to just sit in a specific seat had my indecisive ass looking around for a minute before choosing a window seat on the left side of the plane. Dinero took a seat beside me and a short time later, the pilot came and introduced himself before revealing that we were going to New York, making my eyes buck. I don't know why, but I hadn't been expecting that we were actually going somewhere aside from riding around the city or something before going to dinner. Dinero had yet to make me feel like I was beneath him for being excited about shit he was clearly used to, but I still felt the need to reign it in. So, I didn't immediately start bouncing around in my seat like I really wanted to, and that had him looking my way once the flight crew finished their instructions.

"You cool? I thought you wanted to see New York?" He was trying to keep it in check, but I could hear the underlying concern in his voice.

"Of course! Thank you so much, baby, this gotta be the best night of my life and it ain't even started yet." I bit my lip and sighed, making his smile return.

"You deserve all this and then some, but it's only up from here." Cupping my face, he gave me a kiss that I instantly felt between my legs as the plane ascended.

I swear, flying private was the type of luxury a bitch could get used to, and by the time we landed I didn't even want to get off. Once again, though, Dinero ushered me off to an awaiting car, and I rolled the windows down as we rode through the city so I could see everything, while he pointed out landmarks that he knew from his many times there. He'd kept the night's events to himself, so I didn't even know where we were going until we stopped in front of a building that said Observation Deck. My brows dipped as I looked back at him, unsure of what we were about to do, but I was hoping it involved food because I was starving.

"Maaaan, just trust yo' man, ayite," he drawled as the

driver came around and opened the door, helping me out once again. When Dinero's feet landed on the pavement, he closed my hand in his and walked toward the entrance. I was so busy looking in his damn side profile, though, that I didn't even notice a dirty hand reaching out to me until she'd already grabbed my arm.

"Do you have any change?" My breath caught in my throat just from the sheer surprise, but I quickly calmed down seeing that it was a homeless lady. I wasn't the type that thought I was better than anybody and knew that one decision could knock you right down to rock bottom, so I instantly threw on a smile. It was sad because the girl didn't look very much older than me. Her hair was matted into a sideways ponytail that was full of visible dirt, and her clothes were a few sizes too small and looked just as filthy, and she didn't even have on shoes. By now, Dinero realized that I wasn't trying to move with him and turned to see why.

"Babe, do you have some cash on you?" I looked at him with pleading eyes, and he instantly frowned, ready to turn right back into the man I'd met that very first day. The silence on his end had her head snapping in his direction so that she could ask him directly, but as soon as she laid eyes on him, she gasped and tilted her head to the side in recognition.

"D-Dinero?" I looked back and forth between the two trying to figure out how in the world she would know him and was confused at the expression on his face as he dropped my hand and stepped closer to her.

"What the hell.....Tania?"

To be continued.......

ALSO BY J. DOMINIQUE

Every Savage Deserves A Hood Chick 2

Every Savage Deserves A Hood Chick

Chino And Chanelle

Chino And Chanelle 2

Chino And Chanelle 3

Giving My Heart To A Chi-Town Menace

Giving My Heart To A Chi-Town Menace: Real & Nova Story

Low Key Fallin' For A Savage

Low Key Fallin' For A Savage 2

Low Key Fallin' For A Savage 3

A Hood Love So Real

A Hood Love So Real 2

The Coldest Savage Stole My Heart

The Coldest Savage Stole My Heart 2

Made in the USA
Columbia, SC
04 September 2024

41624381R00093